VAMPTOWN IN THE TIMES OF COVID-19

AF374035

Karen Jane Lewis
VampTown in the Times of Covid-19

All rights reserved
Copyright © 2024 by Karen Jane Lewis

No part of this publication may be reproduced, distributed, or transmitted in any form or by any means, including photocopying, recording, or other electronic or mechanical methods, without the prior written permission of the publisher, except in the case of brief quotations embodied in critical reviews and certain other noncommercial uses permitted by copyright law.

Published by Spines
ISBN: 979-8-89383-541-0

VAMPTOWN IN THE TIMES OF COVID-19

KAREN JANE LEWIS

DEDICATION

This book is affectionately dedicated to my daughters (Angela Solberg, and Jeanmarie Lewis), my son (Anthony Bocchino IV), and my friend (Mark McNary).

CONTENTS

ACKNOWLEDGMENT

With love and gratitude to my wonderful and patient family (especially my children) who supported me while I was writing. Also, special credits to my friend, Marc McNary, who gave me the courage to keep going and taught me the significance of faith in my craft.

CHAPTER I
THE MURKY CLOUD

It's Halloween season!

The day dragged on, giving way to the much-awaited night. 'Tonight, I am a ghost,' Karen thought to herself, 'nocturnal and shrouded, much like the dead I aspire to be.' Belonging to a Goth family, she had always looked up to Halloween more than Christmas. Her parents died due to a car accident – that's what people said and loathed her grandma, Laura, who had always told a different story. "Your parents died saving the vampires of the cloud realm, honey," she would tell her nephew, Karen.

The neighborhood women often bad-mouthed Laura amid their concerns for Karen and believed that she wasn't in a stable mental state to raise her granddaughter well. And rightly so, Laura had her odd ways of doing things – uncanny even. Besides her nocturnal routine – sleep all morning and awake all night – she had often spat on women during the community gathering accusing them of being a member of the Tronox tribe. The one she believed killed her son and daughter-in-law during the war between vampires and humans. Unlike others, Karen had always believed her stories and struggled to follow the ordinary routine too, but to no avail. The only occasion she looked up to throughout the year was Halloween, where there were no gifts or special meals to prepare.

Geeky in nature, she would bunk all the classes and quietly snuck to the library, reading scary stories. At home, her granny would cook a lot of candies for her to pig out for breakfast, and on her way home from school, she would treat herself to a spiced pumpkin latte from her favorite coffee bar. Though she wasn't a party animal, yet on Halloween parties thrown by her school societies, she would dress up like a ghoul and party the night away, grooving like a lunatic till her feet gave up. Only stacked with a hundred shades of black, her wardrobe never failed to present multiple spooky outfits for the party. Hours before the event, she would excitedly make wounds with her special effects makeup kit. That week she had back-to-back three Halloween parties to attend, thanks to the I-can-do-it-better competition between different student societies of her school.

The first party arranged by the Entertainment Society was to be commenced that night. Excited as always, Karen wore the maleficent robe, fixed the rodent fangs on her teeth grazing over her painted red lips, and powdered her face white. As a lover of long strolls, she always preferred walking to places on foot. This Halloween party was already thrown in the Dixon club, which was hardly fifteen minutes walk from her home, so taking her bicycle was out of the question. Dressed up like a zombie, she stepped out of the house. The Halloween sun had set in the city of Alabama, and it was apparent from the candy wrappers blowing over the leaf-strewn sidewalk. For Karen, it wasn't about chocolates or lollipops; rather, the joy attached to the nocturnal and spooky world. 'Tonight, the world is my stage as I feed on the drama through my skin,' she thought. She walked chin up, head high, arms moving out like she was conducting the clouds above.

In no time, the Dixon club slid into view. Hordes of eerie-looking and hideously costumed students were seen swarming inside. In the distance, faint blares of the song "She Wolf" by Sia could be heard coming from the club. Karen excitedly leaped inside and felt like she had entered a different world. The inside of the club was dipped in red light. There was a dance floor in the middle, and the edges were stacked with a bartender pouring out a variety of red drinks to the students seated across from the counter. Six feet above the dance floor was a small compartment, and sitting on what looked like a DJ balcony was a white-skinned guy, playing the disc jockey and making the high schoolers groove over his beat.

Karen was taken aback by the great management – from the ambiance to the music and variety of drinks; everything was spot on. Unlike the previous year, where the members of the Music society deliberately ruined their program so that no one can steal their best organizer award. This time around, the members of this or any other society weren't allowed. Only the students with the loyalty card Entertainment society were allowed inside.

The next minute, a voice on the speaker announced the best-dressed lad and lassie, and the party proceeded with full energy. Karen, too, worked loose and let her body rock on the beat. Without being drunk, she was high on music and danced like there was no one watching. Suddenly, some shady people wearing the Batman mask started pushing girls and boys. In no time, they all scattered over the place and started disturbing everyone at the party. Some of them reached the bartender and began spilling the drinks in the basin. The other Batman-veiled men forced some of the boys and girls sitting on the table to stand up and settled down in their place. One of the guys tried to force himself on a girl who suddenly started yelling at him. The music stopped, and the lights were turned on.

"What's happening here?" Liam – the secretary president of the Entertainment society, broke in. "This guy is misbehaving with me," said Lena – the famous singer of the school. "Bloody freak. Who the hell are you?" spat Liam while pulling out the mask of the guy.

The mask unveiled Peter – the member of the Music Society, and everyone knew what he was there for. Last year as well, he deliberately broke into the Halloween party thrown by the Entertainment society just to ruin their event and steal their members. Surprisingly, some of them did due to the terror and false threats of Peter. Karen didn't, though. She had a habit of leaving the party whenever Peter and his army broke in because she knew what follows after – the fight scene, and she didn't have time for all that so this time as well, she left. She paced outside from the main exit, mouthing curse words at herself.

"How do I always convince myself last minute to attend the school Halloween parties?" she spat. "How could you be so stupid thinking that it won't happen this time too? Damn, I'd have rather stayed at home and read Stephen King to get the gruesome feel than attend this failed-Halloween themed party."

From the jam-packed hordes of the semi-spooky crowd, she stepped into the abandoned lane of the people-less street where hardly two street lamps cast a dim and yellow light on the sad features of the club. The weather was cold even for the end of October as if the warmth of the surrounding had been sucked in by the night sky. It was 2:00 a.m. The hustle of the city was swallowed up by the ghost of silence as midnight fell on the north of Alabama. On the sky, the scud of murky clouds enveloped the black vastness of the sky, and a white-furred wolf resting on a thick canopy awaited the clouds to unveil a glimpse of the moon. The wailing of the siren and hooting of the owls could be heard somewhere in the distance.

The Dixon club was located across from a haunted park, and Jessica − the president of this club, deliberately chose this location to add more impact to the horrendous feel of it. And rightly so, since the venue did augment the level of horror of some students owing to the haunted stories associated with the place. Hardly seven minutes' walk from the club was a thick forest of Conecuh where most of the wild beasts are assumed to be looming around. Unlike others, Karen never dreaded such stories, but in fact, enjoyed them and didn't give aforethought before resolving to walk home at such a crucial time of the night. She angrily made her way down the sidewalk, stomping over the dried autumn leaves, which made a distinct sound.

With each stride she took, the darkness grew even thicker, leaving barely enough light for the shadows to be visible, let alone the paranormal. These were the streets she had walked her entire life, be it mornings, afternoons, or late at night. Its route and scenery had been etched in her head like a carving that she could even walk home blindfolded. After listening to the haunted stories of this lane by her grandmother, she had grown a strange fascination for it. To the extent that, unlike others, she had always found her sanity in times of anger and frustration on this street. Not tonight, though.

Across the park cut ten minutes off her trip home, she sensed something odd in the atmosphere. A weird smell of blood entered her system and made her stop abruptly. For once, she suspected it to be society's plan to scare them and walked on when one lamppost started blinking. Two more of them blinked and went out; it went on till the only in the entire street was the yellow flicker from within the garish jack-o-lanterns. Karen stopped again midway and looked around, but there was no trace of a person on the street. That very instant, a swish of a cool breeze wafted and made Karen rub her forearms.

"Who's there?" she called out.

Nothing but the deafening silence roared back. She continued treading down the sidewalk again when the gnarled tree branches stooped low and started pulling her hair and clothes. She looked up in an instant and found her black wavy hair tangled up with the branches. With a quick reflex, she whisked them off when she caught sight of spider webs strewn over the branches.

"Darn!" she uttered and shuddered away from underneath the ghostly tree. Something in the air felt like the blaring of a death trumpet. The sudden drop in temperature and descent of rustling noise brought Karen's senses to wake. She felt something moving overhead and craned her neck to look up.

Right before her eyes, she watched as one candy-floss grey cloud attracted all other puffy clouds towards it till the point when the sky unraveled a blood-red moon and all the stars from underneath it. The first glimpse of the moon made the desperate wolves howl their vocals out. In no time, this candy-floss cloud turned into a thick cocoon of grey velvet and started drifting across the vastness of the sky.

Karen bawled out her eyes over the uncanny sight.

"What is that?" she blurted out and looked around but couldn't find anyone to exchange interrogating glances on the unusual appeal of the cloud. The very next minute, this cloud of murk took a sudden halt right above her. Frozen in her spot, she ghastly looked at the oddest cloud she had ever seen—a large mammatus puff with many small pouchy formations. The foul air emanated by this misty cloud gave the nearby vicinity a tincture that Karen associated with the warning before a storm. She watched as it loomed nearer to the ground. Consumed by panic, she looked around again, hoping someone was there witnessing it with her, but the streets showed no sign of homo sapiens. Feeling her first wave of nerve, she broke into a run. The absolute silence of the thick cocoon of cloud was replaced by a rustling sound of the winds singing a terror-ridden lullaby. Karen dashed forth akin a prey running for his dear life. She craned her neck up again and realized for the first time how hard it is to maintain pace while running face-up to the sky. The sinister cloud seemed to imitate her stride diagonally coming down for her. From the predator cloud came the sounds that ebbed and flowed much like waves on the moonlit sand. With her heart thudding in her chest, she strained to listen against the whooshing winds the unintelligible words coming from the uncanny cloud. It was certainly no language she knew, but the hissing sounded like a foreign language.

Regardless of how fast Karen swept, the cloud was advancing towards her with twice the speed. As the time elapsed, the mammatus puff of cloud took the shape of a lenticular tornado and started rolling towards her. The winds blew cold on her and started numbing her limbs. The black muddy twister devours one fall, and her. She glanced over her shoulder and almost tasted cold mud. While running with her head turned to face the tornado, she didn't notice the yellow beams of the car. The rushing sound of the tornado drowned out the honks of the car. The only next sound was the screeches of the brakes and screams of Karen. The car came to a halt two inches before hitting her. The car driver happened to be a man in his fifties who slid down his window and started berating her.

"What's wrong with you, lady? I've been flashing the headlights and buzzing the horn for so long for you to notice. Can't you hear or see? Why are you running like a freak?"

"I'm so sorry," she panted. "It is this cloud of tornado chasing me for –" she whipped around to point at it, but to her surprise, it was gone.

"Are you drunk?" squealed the angry man. "Go home now. Don't waste my time." With a press of a button, he slid up the car windows and ruthlessly drove past her. Karen was paralyzed in her spot for a while. Bedraggled and swallowing down the thick lump formed in her throat, she hesitantly looked up and around to find the traces of that grisly cloud. To her relief, it wasn't anywhere around. With panic still flaring inside her, she quickly dashed towards her home. She had hardly taken five peaceful breaths before that swirl of Mammatus cloud appeared again, but this time in the distance. This cloud had now scattered over the Contech forest, and the very next minute, it started disfiguring into the same tornado. In no time, she watched as this tornado fired multiple thunderbolts in different regions of Alabama.

Something inside her shifted, and she didn't know what. After experiencing the close call when her body should be preparing for a fight or flight response, it is glued to the spot. Instead of running away, she was consumed with curiosity and watching wide-eyed at the unseen. The thunderbolts she saw were different in color. They fired like red streaks in different directions of the Contech forest. Almost a minute after the thunderbolt, she heard screams and wails. Every snap of a twig felt like that of a predator. She felt her ears growing sharper and her mind getting paranoid. For the time that followed, she almost forgot how to move her joints.

The red moonlight sucked in the green of the forest and draped it in the velvet of red through rusty rays. The violent streaks of thunder bolting across the air made the atmosphere colder than ice. Swimming out of her curiosity,

when Karen attempted to walk with frozen muscles, she watched a thunderous red flicker nearby. Something about it made her paralyzed in her spot. It wasn't a flicker, but rather a bolting apparition. A minute later followed the ear-screeching scream of a lady that made the nightingales take wing in the woods. The howling wolves, hooting owls, and chirping squirrels immediately went mute, and the lights of every nearby household flicked on. Some men and women came out of their houses oblivious of what had happened; others tried to gauge the direction of the scream. Two minutes later, they all went inside and shut their doors behind the mournful night.

CHAPTER 2
SWOOSH OF WINDS

2nd December 2016.

Midnight fell like a rich velvet of black and draped the green forest of Conecuh into grim and grisly coal. The pitch-black sky of vastness sprawled its arms wide, willing to devour any speck of light imminent in the Alabama city. Meanwhile, the humans laid sound asleep, and empty streets exhibited abandonment in their demeanor.

Far and wide, the darkness was so prominent in the scene that only the smattering of luminous stars lent the little light the city could get. The sky was void of the moon, and the wolves whimpered in a low pitch, awaiting its sight. Amidst the horrendous silence looming across the city, even the rustling of leaves and whisper of the winds sounded thunderous. If someone woke up in the middle of the night, they would even be able to hear a beetle tottering across the earth. Such was the level of acute hearing accredited to the deadly silence.

Across from the forest laid a road like a tarmac ribbon, one that had been worn over time. A white line running across the center appeared relatively unbroken when compared with the scarred and potholed concrete. Whooshing down this road in a haphazard direction was a cabriolet car – the only vehicle visible in the wide stretch of the lane. Mia and her husband Miles were sitting in the car, enjoying the drive like reckless teenagers. As only married some weeks ago, the duo hadn't given up on the mindset of careless youngsters in them. Miles, madly in love with his wife, seemed to fulfill all her desires and provide her with things before she could even mouth her demands.

For the same reason, just when Mia requested for going on a long drive in the middle of the night, Miles couldn't refuse her. Therefore, without much thought, the much-in-love couple set out on an adventure across the restricted lane of the Conecuh Forest. Unlike this duo, people had dreaded driving to the ghastly edge of the Conecuh Forest because of its associated haunted stories.

Mia, on the other hand, had an uncanny interest in the paranormal since her school days. She had highly been recognized for her fearless and dauntless attitude. She would often accept the challenges of staying alone for hours in the old haunted house, and library, and won cash over the bet. When single, she used to visit such areas alone. Now married, she convinced her husband as well into becoming a part of her daring activities. A week earlier, the duo completed the challenge of watching the 'Hereditary' movie alone in the cinema and got a monetary reward from the movie director himself. Having done that much together, a mere trek down the haunted lane didn't seem that much of a problem to them.

Growing up in the outskirts of Alabama, Mia had each haunted tale concerning the horrific incidents of the Conecuh Forest memorized by heart. One in which a group of five foreigners camping in the woods went missing a year ago. Another one was where two blood-soaked bodies of college friends were found hanging upside down on the Balete tree. Mia had heard these stories so many times that they stopped impacting her that way.

After giving his wife a good tour of almost the entire town, Miles – upon Mia's request, geared his car down the Conecuh Road. The quiet stretch of the road lining the woods echoed with the rushing sound of their car. Unconcerned about midnight and enjoying the ride to the fullest, Mia hooted and laughed throughout the night. "C'mon, monstrous creatures. Where are you hiding?" Mia exclaimed at the top of her lungs. "What are you doing, honey?" giggled Miles.

"Calling for the ghosts residing in the woods," she announced, snorting all the while hysterically. "C'mon apparitions. Get out of your caves. Your meal is right here."

"Not sure about the ghosts, but you'll sure as hell wake the animals and other nearby residents," he smirked.

"So be it," blabbered Mia, throwing away the empty bottle of gin.

Miles realized that his wife was boozy and chuckled at her adoringly. "Alright, baby, you will be gone any minute now, I presume. This is the last lane we're taking on your request, and then we'll get back home."

"Oh, no. No," she muttered. "I'm all vigilant. See," she leaned in and widely opened her eyes for her husband to see.

Miles looked at his wife as she leaned in closer and pouted her lips out. Watching her stupidity affectionately, he also propped her closer to give her a kiss when his car went out of control and bumped into a big Balete tree.

"Ouch," Mia let out, rubbing her forehead. "You okay, honey," Miles asked, concerned. He watched as a small cut ran across her wife's forehead, making it bleed. "Oh, shit."

"It's okay," mumbled Mia while running her finger along the area of sharp pain and sensing the size of the bruise.

Miles tossed glances between his wife and the car, which was in shambles from the front. Upon catching his husband watching her out of concern, Mia uttered, "I'm fine, Miles." Her eyes fell on the badly scrunched bonnet, "how are we going to go home now?" she asked.

Miles trundled out of his vehicle and walked around to check for the damage. He hauled up the bonnet with all his force as the engine emitted a large puff of smoke. Coughing hard, he waved away the smoke and checked for the broken wires. Mia remained seated there for a while and watched as her husband struggled in vain to fix the car. "What are we going to do now?" she muttered.

"I don't know. Let me see −" He stopped studying the wires and quickly said, "wait! I know how to get this thing started." Slumping back in her seat, Mia grumbled, "But how long will it take? I'm sleepy." "Not that long," Miles smiled.

"Okay," she said. While sitting in the car for more than five minutes, Mia's felt something moving overhead.

With a quick reflex, her eyes fell on the sky. "Miles. What is that?" she asked curiously.

Stopping midway from work, Miles looked up and saw the grey candy-floss clouds attracting all other puffy clouds towards it. "I don't know," he replied and got back to fixing the wires. Mia had her eyes affixed on the magnetic cloud attracting all other puffs and unraveling the blood-red moon and all the stars from underneath it. Mindlessly, she climbed out of the car and started following the cloud, which seemed to be heading toward the forest. Already a lover of the uncanny, she watched astonishingly at the grey cloud buzzing with weird energy. While Miles kept talking about the wires, Mia silently darted off into the thick of woods. She squinted at the appeal of the sinister clouds, which started taking the shape of a lenticular tornado. She watched as a flicker of light fired out of the cloud and struck somewhere deep in the forest. Then followed a painful yelp of the wolf. The mere sound of the creature made shivers run down her spine.

Feeling her first wave of nerve, Mia exclaimed, "Miles! Look at that —" she looked around and realized she had left her husband behind and come too far following the cloud. Contemplating for a moment, whether to go back or follow the howl, she chose the latter. She strode deeper into the woods, all the while concerned about the wolf that got struck by a thunderbolt. Plodding on, her eyes fell on the sinister cloud, which started imitating her stride and began coming down for her diagonally. Feeling her heart bludgeoning in her chest, she broke into a run. The predator cloud started matching her pace, and from inside came the sound of incoherent mumbles. Mia strained her ears, but the language sounded alien yet clear. The winds blew cold on her and started numbing her limbs. Pacing at full speed, Mia kept getting tangled up with droopy branches of gnarled trees hanging overhead. "Miles!" she struggled to find her voice, but nothing came above an inaudible mumble. The forest grew darker and thicker. Her feet crunched the lifeless bushes as she dashed forth at an insane pace. The wailing of the siren and hooting of the owls grew louder far away. The blood moon reigning the ruddy red sky sucked in the warmth of the air, leaving it crisp and cold. She sprinted forth, breaking a cold sweat, dreading the lenticular cloud, which pounded with twice her speed. The next minute, she spotted a flicker bolting in the distance. The blood moon sent an infusion of bloody air across the island, and Mia could smell blood in the air. The red moonlight sucked in the green of the forest and draped it in the velvet of red through rusty rays. Just then, while Mia was busy looking over her shoulder, a bolt of light whooshed past her and transfigured into a grotesque apparition before her. A bloodless and ivory-white creature slid into view with ears, wings, and rodent fangs like a bat and white eyes, a crooked nose of a corpse. Its tongue lolled to one side upon watching her forehead bruise dripping blood. Disheveled and fretful, Mia finally let out a scream, "Miles!" Miles, who was busy connecting the wires, suddenly looked up. "Mia," he mouthed, oblivious that she was gone all this time. He looked around, but she was nowhere. "Mia!" he called out again, louder this time. In the woods, Mia heard him yet couldn't help but run deeper into the woods, escaping the nocturnal creature that bolted after her at the speed of light. "Miles!" she yelled back before the rodent monster could catch up. Her husband, who was looking for her signs at the road, whipped around and gauged the direction of her voice coming from the woods. He scurried after her in that direction, stomping on the dried leaves, making a specific crunching sound. The forest was dark and maze-like. He kept pacing, unsure where he was heading, but thinking that his wife must be in trouble, he trod down the dark forest. Every time he called out for his wife, his voice echoed into the void. He looked up and saw a huge spaceship-like cloud advancing eastwards. Bawling his eyes out at the strangeness of the cloud, he recalled exactly when he must have lost his wife.

"Now that's the culprit," he grumbled, and started following it to know the whereabouts of Mia. The semi-red moon, now completely turned into blood, stopped lending the little light it could spare. Concerned about his wife, he took long desperate steps in the direction of the cloud and broke into a run as the cloud started rotating at the speed of a tornado. Sprinting for it and struggling to breathe in the cold, he tripped on something flesh-like. He sensed as his hand touched a dry, furry body. Squinting in the absolute darkness, Miles conjured up the sight of a wheezing, injured wolf. The lower bottom of the creature looked thunder-burned, revealing pink flesh, bleeding profoundly.

"Oh my God," cried Miles, stepping back in an instant with shock. His thoughts and concern were switching immediately to Mia, fathoming the state she would be in. After giving a slight pat over the wolf's head, who was breathing its last, he rose to his feet and began chasing the cloud again. "Mia!" he called out again. Just then, he watched two other flickers falling diagonally to the ground in the distance.

On the other hand, Mia wriggled and flailed her way ahead, her energy giving in to the booze she had had earlier on the long drive. Her legs were still trained on running, oblivious of no other way to escape the nightmare. Over the sound of rustling winds and indistinctive mumbling coming from the lenticular cloud, she could hardly hear Miles' voice. Three flashes of light kept buzzing around her. Despite the close range and unearthly speed, the rodent apparitions kept whizzing back and forth in haphazard directions.

Mia felt the thorns beginning to form in her throat out of thirst. Her eyes started getting droopy, and she resisted the urge to sit or lay down right there. Out in the distance, her eyes fell on an open space with comparatively fewer trees surrounding its territory. From a distance and already dark as it was, it looked like an exit leading to the service lane of Conecuh. A speck of hope was instilled in Mia as she encouraged herself to make it that far. With wobbly feet, she tottered in that direction as fast as she could. Swallowing down the lump in her throat, she looked over her shoulder and found three of those hideous creatures following her. Where Mia was running, those three apparitions only took long strides to match her pace. Their semi-human lips were curled up in a triumphant grin, and their eyes fixated on her forehead bruise. Mia gulped down the little dampness her tongue could forge and rubbed her arms as the winds blew cold on her. With panic flaring inside her and prickles swarming beneath her clothes, she paced on till she reached the threshold. To her surprise, what looked like an exit from afar was, in fact, a large quarry. The insides of this round yet deep well were stacked with hordes of pale-white bodies lying chaotically. Mia's eyes bawled out of her socket over the horrific sight. There was no way out. In front of her was a hundred feet deep quarry, and behind her, the apparitions stood smiling. Death loomed from all corners. She wheeled around and pleaded, "Please, don't kill me." The hideous creatures exchanged a mocking smirk with one another and advanced toward her. The next minute, an ear-splitting scream numbed Miles' senses. The same yelp made the howling wolves, hooting owls, and chirping squirrels go mute. A mile away from the forest, Karen froze in her spot, terrorized by the sound. The painful shriek woke up every individual living in a colony at a one-mile radius and dragged them out of their houses.

CHAPTER 3
THE VAMPIRE RAVE

"Ah! The Battle of Trinix. One of the deadliest battles ever fought between the cold-blooded and warm-blooded species. It still brings goosebumps when I think about it. A clash in which the Goths proved their loyalty to the cold-blooded Vampires and fought with blood and sweat against the warm-blooded animals. Your parents lost their lives on the same battlefield and won the trust of Lord Byron — the former ruler of Vamp Town. I was there as well; watched it very closely as the battleground became the blood-soaking arena. Earlier that day, the combat zone had a cold malevolent air to it — a plus point for the Vampires who could burn to death in the presence of sunlight. The winds had no direction in the foothills of Bayford as if fathoming the cause of the ceasefire between the warm-blooded species (led by the Tronox tribe) and cold-blooded species (led by Lord Byron).

As far as the sight could reach, there were bodies all across the ground baked in dust and dirt. You could tell apart the bodies of cold-blooded Vampires from warm-blooded humans. The blood-soaked corpses with some kind of mucus-secreting out of their bodies were the Vampires while the pale-white bodies lying in the pool of their blood were humans except that some of them were Goths. Till that point, lives were equally lost from both sides, and one couldn't predict who was going to win this one. I was sitting at a camp in the distance, carrying you in my arms and concerned about your father and mother. Every face depicted a clear sign of exhaustion. The humans wore metal armor all around their bodies to prevent the attack as well as the smell of blood from reaching the Vampires' senses, and so did Vampires to protect themselves from sunlight. Amidst the face-off, a sudden infusion of fog rolled into the atmosphere, blurring up the scene. Where one minute, the steel was clashing against steel, and bullets and arrows were drizzling down on both sides; the next minute, there was nothing. The fog was dense; none could see through it except the Vampires with their special power. Considering the coolness exuded by the fog, the warm-blooded army suspected it was a strategy of the Vampires and hesitated in throwing themselves into the fray. Whereas, the Vampires who were already accustomed to seeing through more or less similar fog strode forward fearlessly, reckoning it to be nature's help. And I thanked God, thinking that your parents would be deemed victorious together with Lord Byron, but I was wrong. Across the battleground, I could hear the bloodcurdling echoes of the blades penetrating through the armor and flesh of the humans as the Vampires took over them. The fog got thicker, making it impossible for the warm-blooded species to even stand in their *defense. They swished their swords in the air, slicing through the fog but to no avail as more of the members of the Tronox tribe were getting injured or sliced in the process. The air was thick with the aroma of iron, blood soaking in every inch of human's armor and skin from the massacre within the fog, infusing a foul stench and causing some of the humans to heave and vampires to crave for blood. Both the opponents settled down for a moment to breathe when suddenly, a speck of ray emerged from behind the hazy fog. A minute later, some more rays befell the battleground and swallowed all the smog, bringing the Tronox and Lord Byron's tribe face to face. For the next fifteen minutes, the battle continued at its full ferocity, and the white-blooded army lost many lives till the point the unrelenting sun secured its' place above the horizon. It was then the table turned. To the surprise of both the homo sapiens and Vampires, the sun began projecting its merciless rays down on the Conecuh city and made the battlefield a gladiator's arena. The temperature rose to the point that even the armor of the cold-blooded species started melting on their skin. The humans still declared it the hottest summer day ever. They took off their armor and fought till the end despite the skin patches. The next minute, some ear-splitting roars of the bats met everyone's ears as the cold-blooded species shrieked in pain. The Vampires weren't aware of the penetrating nature of steel in the face of heat and began melting down along with their armor. Watching half of their tribe dripping down like molten lava, the Goths fought with everything in their power. Since only being a quarter the size of the Tronox army, they were immediately outnumbered and brutally slain to death. Before the battle, Lord*

Byron's army had very smartly installed an alarm system sensitive to the rise in temperature, which was connected to the cloud shuttles. To its efficiency, the system accurately blared a warning, calling the cold-blooded species for retreat except that its sound was drowned out by the painful groaning of the Vampires. The signal sensors also launched the cloud shuttles on the edge of the battleground; only those rodents who heard the siren wailing and were fighting near the edge got on the shuttles and set off to the murky cloud. As for me, I clutched onto my prayer beads and began reciting a hymn in an attempt to send prayers to my son and daughter-in-law, begging God to spare their life but to no avail. Right then, a hand suddenly grabbed hold of my arm, snapping me out of my chants, and nudged me to retreat. It was Lord Byron — the Knight himself."

Had he done that on regular days, I would have bent down before your majesty over his kind concern, but given the situation in consideration, I was not in my senses. I let go of my hand from his in a snap and asked him about Bella and James. You were whining more loudly then. Lord Byron's eyes fell on you and then rose to meet mine. I still remember his words as he said, "they've proven their loyalty with the Byron tribe, so it's my noblesse oblige to rescue their mother and daughter now." I knew what he meant, and I collapsed to my knees out of shock. He immediately grabbed you from my lap, or you could've fallen with me. "Control yourself, Laura. We need to get out of here; you have to think about your granddaughter." Byron had this prominent eye patch and grizzly hazelnut-toned beard. Watching the white-blooded army coming for us, he immediately got my hand and *dragged me along, much like a ragdoll before I finally compiled myself and matched pace with him, ignoring the blood that oozed out of my knees and slowed down my pace. We darted towards the cloud shuttle while the humans sprinted for us. The next minute, we were in the shuttle along with other survivors, gasping in pain as Medics hurry around each individual to aid them. Then it dawned on me how if it hadn't been for Lord Byron to drag me from the camp, we would've been slaughtered with the rest or reanimated as servants to the usurpers. Then I urged my apology and showed my gratitude for his kind gesture and decided to pay him back for his heroism. Initially, all the Goths resided on the murky cloud, but later it became hard for them to survive in the bone-chilling temperature. Furthermore, the Vampires couldn't hold back their temptations and craved the human blood running in their veins; therefore, Lord Byron decided to send the Goths back down to earth and lead a safe life. "And we are here," Laura smiled.*

Karen had listened to this story a thousand times from her grandmother; she even had it memorized by heart. It was always the same details; nothing more, nothing less. Despite that, she listened to it with the same interest as if hearing it for the first time. She loved it when her granny sounded all sane and sound. While Laura, on the other hand, hadn't gotten over his son and daughter-in-law's death, and it was evident from her mental state and random fits of insanity.

Yet she always seemed to speak with conviction and

confidence when narrating the old happenings. Karen had always believed her. Many neighborhood women asked her not to believe her stories and submit herself in safer custody considering Laura's mental condition, but she never paid heed to any of them. After residing with her granny for great eighteen years, she could tell apart between her normalcy and insanity – her truth and hallucinatory stories. Other than that, since morning, Karen had been sensing a disturbing oddity in the air. She had her mind budget for a while from her doomy walk home last night because of her granny's story, but it started going back there. She couldn't tell Laura what she witnessed last night, dreading another burst of energy from her side. Even when she attempted to forget about it, the sinister feel in the atmosphere – the one she felt when the murky cloud followed her, reminded her of the mystical presence. Just like her parents, Karen possessed super active senses that were sensitive to the slightest uncanny changes in the atmosphere; she could easily predict rainfall, tornado, tsunami, eclipse, and all such natural occurring. This time around, she could smell blood in the air and couldn't shake off the shrieks of Mia she heard the night before. Dressed in her favorite pitch-black dress, ready to set off for high school, Karen always found some time to sit by her granny's side at the kitchen table while having breakfast and hearing her out before leaving. She did the same that day as well. The only difference this time around was, most of what Laura said synced with reality. Perhaps because Karen had had a paranormal episode the night before, she felt the story differently this time. Her Goth blood began to gurgle within her skin and gave her rashes, something that had never happened before. Having a strong fascination for the paranormal and nocturnal routine, Karen had usually enjoyed tales related to supernatural occurrences. Still, after experiencing what she had the night before, she developed a snooping curiosity for the uncanny and pined to unravel it. After munching on the scrambled egg and toasts and kissing her granny goodbye, who was already dozing off at intervals owing to her nocturnal routine, Karen left for her school. Emerging from her home into the day glare, Karen's senses involuntarily became vigilant. The more distance she covered away from home, the more she felt a temperature drop in her bones. There was no trace of the sun in the sky, and the streets were as void as the night before. The winds gusted cold gushes on her, making her sway in different directions. Despite the otherwise stormy forecast, Karen's senses fathomed the paranormal presence in her city. As far as her sight could stretch, there was no activity on the street – not even a stray cat or dog tumbling past in the distance. A thought of being left alone on the planet crossed her mind.

The morning exhibited the view of misty, cold dusk, and the chilly winds carried the scents of rain. In the sky, the clouds were arranged as neatly as a child's toys stacked back in place by his mother. Perfect greyish puffs drifted overhead, suggesting a long, mild storm. Karen strolled as quickly as she could to escape the cold and the people-less street she wasn't used to witnessing. Hardly after the ten minutes walk, the sight of some familiar faces strolling in the direction of school lent her some sighs of relief. The red-bricked building that read Hawkeye Secondary High School was derelict in comparison with the neighborhood bungalows, which were mostly refurbished. Next to the well-maintained and fancy architecture, the three-story high school building looked like the one extracted from a horror movie set, so dilapidated that an untouched structure could expect nothing good, so beaten down by endless seasons of weathering. Some of the windows were broken, and the ones that stayed in their place were grey with the grime of twenty years. The insides of the school had rotten stairways where a few incidents of the students' falls were recorded. The walls had peeled off wallpapers, and some black and white photographs of what seemed like the owner's father were stacked on the walls along with some photostat quotes. The building itself, with its derelict appeal, looked like it was being passed on from generation to generation. No one knew who owned it and why it hadn't been either demolished or refurbished. Located on a hill, the school was renowned for its perfect haunted nature. At night, people had even witnessed some flickering lights at some of the windows. The students were now used to it, but initially, when the winds blew right in, the corridor whistles would give cringes to every student. Only those who had a love for the uncanny or were extremely daring took pride in telling their friends and relatives about getting admitted to Hawkeye High School. Karen, Goth by nature, was already fond of all the spooky things, and Laura couldn't help but swoon over her granddaughter for having similar interests as her father, James. Most of the students studying in this college were looked up to and deemed 'cooler' by other High Schoolers because of their dauntless nature and adventurous spirit. The principal of this college, Mr. Jackal Patterson also had an element of eccentricity to him. Rumors had it that he had three encounters with demons in this college when he took charge of the place. Since that happened, he'd become quieter, but whenever he spoke, he'd spat after completing a sentence. The young, black guy responsible for mopping and cleaning was mostly found in his office and around his corridor because of the pool he created in that area. Karen swarmed inside with a bunch of other familiar faces and found her best friend, Sophia Miller, in the hallway. "Hey, Sophie!" she called out. A girl with black straight hair flipped around and beamed at Karen. Sophie had pale white skin highlighted over the goofy cat-eyed spectacles she wore. "Hi, Karen." She looked at her watch and said, "I waited for almost fifteen minutes before coming inside. What took you so long?" "I'm sorry. It's this street – did you notice Dixon Lane street today?" Karen asked curiously. "Not really," Sophie said and rose a thick horror novel she was reading. "Was delved into this book. Also, Paa dropped me here, so staring at the same boring street was out of the question." Karen looked at the book that read, 'Horror story 3', and rolled her eyes. "Oh, come on, what has happened to your collection? It isn't even near to spooky, this thing." She heaved an annoying sigh. "Dude, I like it so far. Could you please let me enjoy the read without being nosy or a spoiler for that matter," said Sophie sarcastically. "Alright. Alright." Karen held her hands up in defense. "Go on. Then don't come to me whining about wasting your time on this one." "I won't," said Sophie confidently. "Anyways, forget that. Do you tell? How was the Halloween party? Did the entertainment society do well this time?" "Oh, don't ask," said Karen, annoyance apparent in her demeanor yet struggling to hide it from her friend. "Whoa," Sophie erupted into laughter. "Don't tell me Peter broke in again." She looked at Karen, who gazed at her from the corner of her eye and started walking fast so that Sophie couldn't catch up. "Hahahaha…Damn! See, didn't I tell you that earlier? Told you not to come whining-about-wasting-your-time-on-this-one," she mimicked Karen and hugged her from behind. Karen struggled to let go of her grip with a shove, but Sophie held on tightly. "Let me go…" she mockingly whined. "Not until you buy me grilled chicken from Buttery Eatery, as you started the bet," Sophie grinned. "Urgh. I'm broke," Karen chanted. "Should've thought before deciding on a bet," Sophie threw her hands her Karen and nudged her towards the classroom. "Alright," said Karen weakly, "but on one condition," her eyes widened with excitement. "What, now?" asked Sophie.

"You're going to survey the woods with me on our way to Buttery Eatery," said Karen energetically. "Deal done?"

"What woods? The Conecuh forests?"

"Yesss!" exclaimed Karen.

"Done. Just make sure that we reach Buttery Eatery before the shutters are down," Sophie warned.

"Don't you worry, mate," Karen winked.

Upon clambering up the hallway stairs, Karen and Sophie heard the hooting of boys and girls coming from the first floor.

"Now, what's that?" Sophie blurted out while climbing up the stairs quickly.

Karen frowned in confusion, wondering what that could be for when she heard someone saying, "We don't talk to ugly secretaries here. Where's the pretty president?" and burst into a croaky laugh.

"Oh, I know what's going on there," Karen said, recognizing the voice of Peter.

Sophie looked around, watching her friend nodding her head in disapproval, and scurried forward out of curiosity.

In the thick hallway of the first floor with patches of boys and girls on either side, a face-off was going on between Peter – the notorious president of the music society, and Liam – the secretary of the entertainment society.

"Talk about strength; then it's always man vs. man.

Don't drag a woman here," Liam spat.

"Aww… I didn't know that your president couldn't talk for herself," Peter teased. "Anyways, a nice party you arranged," he winked.

Liam's face turned red, and he immediately grabbed Peter's neck. "You're going to pay back for it."

"Oh, my God! Could you guys please stop it? Liam—"

she paced towards him and wrapped her hands around his back, pulling him back. "Leave him, Liam."

Right then, Peter saw Professor Kingsmith popping out his eyes and trying to get through the thick patch of students surrounding the boxing ring. Upon catching his sight, Peter started making choking noises and began muttering, "please, don't do this. I'm choking. You can ruin my Halloween party, but leave me for now."

Liam couldn't believe Peter was saying this. He was about to let go of his neck when Professor Kingsmith pulled Liam from Peter's side and shoved him back.

"Are you in your senses? What do you think you were doing?" Professor Kingsmith rumbled.

"Sir, he started. Last night—"

"Shut up," Professor Kingsmith roared. "Do you think I'm stupid here? I told you not to go aggressive ever again, but now you—being the secretary, are threatening the president of the music society to ruin his event. I'm never going to let the cheaters win. Never. But first, you got to come with me to the principal."

He held Liam by the ear, berated the students to disperse, and dragged Liam to the principal's room. Jennifer followed them anxiously. The students laughed and went back to the classroom. Karen and Sophie secured their place on the front bench and discussed the upcoming horror series of Norway Christopher. Five minutes later, Miss Angelina—the PHP teacher appeared. This was Karen's favorite subject. She had always had a knack for computer programming and had a dab hand in code running. Miss Angelina told students about the biggest competition going to be held among the country's high schools, and the winner will win a trip to the Maldives. Over the mention of this project, both Karen and

Sophie looked at each other with eyes full of wonder. They listed down their name as a team and decided to construct an app that will track and connect all the databases nearby without having to enter the wifi password.

The rest of the lectures weren't as interesting as the PHP, yet Karen and Sophie, geeks by nature, jotted down all the points and made notes of what the professors had to teach. After the college premises, the best friends did as planned. They took the route down the Conecuh Forest, hardly ten minutes away from the Buttery Eatery restaurant. On her way, Karen told Sophie about the last night's incident; how she saw a murky puffy cloud that followed her and ultimately ended up at the Conecuh Forest together with the screams of a woman.

"I read that in the newspaper in the morning. His husband, Miles, covered the same story. He thinks she went missing," said Sophie.

"I think she must be dead," reported Karen with confidence.

In the bright afternoon, both Karen and Sophie went into the woods and looked at the sash bordering a region that read 'crime scene – do not enter.' Both the friends looked at each other, and their lips curled up in a grin. They held hands and stomped on the sash and strode forth. Halfway through the woods, they saw clotted blood on the ground behind the bushes.

"Whoa. Is that where she died?" Sophie asked.

"I don't think so," said a voice from behind. It was a burly inspector looking furiously at them. "What are you girls doing around here?" he coldly interrogated.

"Nothing. Just looking for her—um, my wristwatch I forgot the other day," Karen blurted out.

"Do you know who could forget his/her wristwatch here?" the inspector asked suspiciously. Karen and Sophie

shook their head in disapproval. "Someone who's involved in the crime scene," he said coldly.

"Oh, no. No. We aren't. I'm so sorry, sir. We were just two detective aspirants to try our luck here. So sorry," Sophie said hesitantly.

"Then vacate," the inspector said, curtly.

Karen and Sophie quickly darted towards the exit and didn't stop before the Buttery Eatery restaurant came into view. Sophie narrowed her eyes upon finding the shutters of the restaurant closed and looked at Karen furiously. Karen guiltily looked at her friend and mouthed barely above a mumble, "Sorry."

Sophie started pacing down the road, taking her route towards her home when Karen skidded her to stop midway.

"Dear, I'm sorry. You come over to my place; I'll cook you grilled chicken for myself," Karen suggested guiltily.

"I'm not hungry anymore," Sophie said coldly.

"Please," Karen requested. "I swear it's going to be restaurant-flavored grilled chicken, and we'll also run some codes to unlock the nearest database. Sounds exciting?" Sophie smiled. "Okay."

Hardly seven minutes' walk from Buttery Eatery, Karen and Sophie reached home. Karen opened her computer for Sophie to run codes while she cooked grilled chicken in the kitchen. Laura was asleep in her room. Sophie was only able to track and break the lock of three Wi-Fi networks nearby before Karen came forth with delicious grilled chicken garnished with garlic bread and parsley. Sophie munched on the food while Karen tracked multiple networks in an instant while running multiple codes. "Very smart," Sophie uttered, her mouth full of garlic bread.

Karen applied the password breaker and got access to multiple networks. There was one site she couldn't get access to, owing to its strong code setting. "Haha, I bet you can't get access to this one," Sophie muttered while munching down the chicken. "What if I did?" Karen asked. "Lasagna from Buttery Eatery, mate," Sophie bet. "Watch me now," Karen said and applied the final code. "Ta Daa…" she turned to face her friend.

Sophie watched with her mouth open as the Vampire Rave site opened up to the sight of men slicing down women and sipping down their blood. Karen turned around and had her eyes bawling out of her socket.

CHAPTER 4

THE TALK OF VAMPTOWN

Goosebumps crept down Karen's spine like a careful spider leaving a trail of silk. A multitude of emotions gripped her from all sides: thrill, excitement, nervousness, and an inexplicable dread. Amidst the stomach-churning, she wheeled her chair towards the computer and jotted up the courage to replay the video again. As for Sophia, she had her brain shut down. Her wide eyes exhibited fear, and the hair on the nape of her neck bristled. There was a glisten of cold sweat evident on her forehead as she weakly put the plate of grilled chicken down. Karen slowly reached her hand up to the mouse and clicked the replay button.

Both the friends watched in horror a weird collection of videos shared by a guy named Drake with a caption that said, "Challenging my friends @Simba_Alaric @Damien98 and @Blade&Aric to maneuver the trickiest method of slicing humans to extract the juiciest blood. Here's my collection. Take notes."

"Oh, my God! Turn this off. Turn this off. Turn this off," Sophia repeated hysterically. Karen watched her friend lose calm and quickly put the computer on standby.

"Okay-okay. Relax-relax!" Karen comforted her friend. She quickly reached her friend on the bed and took her in an embrace, "It's okay. It's okay."

"Is this…" Sophia paused and swallowed hard. "Is this for real?"

"Seems real," Karen let out, struggling to find the balance in her voice.

"What was that?" Sophia mouthed; her voice still shaky and frail. "Which site is it?" It was just then Karen blankly stared at her friend and realized that she was so taken aback by the mysterious nature of the visual that she didn't even see for herself which website was it. She swung her legs off the bed again and reached for the computer to find out.

"Don't! Not now, please." Sophia requested.

"What the hell, Sophia," Karen almost berated her friend. "Since when have you become this much of a pussy? You're a Goth yourself and read more spooky stuff than this. Come on now." She flicked open the system eagerly and ran the code again, but the site was gone. "What on earth?" She spat and glared at Sophia.

"What?" Sophia timidly looked at her. "Why are you looking at me like that?"

"The site is locked again," Karen retorted. "It's all because of you."

"Oh please. Don't blame me now. You were scared too," Sophia defended. "Also, it'd be better if we don't delve into such sites, or we could get in trouble."

"This isn't trouble!" Karen spat. "And what happened to you? I'm amazed." Sophia looked over at Karen guiltily for a while and suddenly got to her feet. "I think I should leave before night falls." She spared a glance at the wall clock that read 6:30 p.m. and wore her shoes.

"Fine," Karen annoyingly said.

~

Vamp Town

The intruder radar blared at the head office of 'The Vampire Rave.'

"What's happening?" Cancer, the founder of Vampire Rave, said. He looked around and saw one of the red lights flicking on and off. He stood up abruptly and hurried out of his cabin.

Sitting outside, opposite their large computers was a group of programmers. Upon hearing the beeping, they all exhibited frenzy and examined their personal computers to see if they hadn't made a blunder or something. But none of them did. Cancer knew what that meant. He walked over to another cubicle where Lazarus, the manager programmer, was seated.

He flung open the door of Lazarus's room and anxiously said, "Laz! Time to reboot the security programming. A human tried to break into her website."

"I dread the same!" Lazarus said.

With that, both Cancer and Lazarus sat together and strengthened the security settings in haste. Once done, they sighed a breath of relief.

"Cancer?" Lazarus said. "Can't we spot the intruder's location from the database that we've got?"

"We can't track the exact location of the intruder, but we can spot the city and the region in general," Cancer informed.

"Then, we must get a bunch of programmers to upgrade the intruder's tracking location so that we can hack that PC and threaten the one trying to do this," Lazarus stated.

"I think you're right," Cancer agreed. "Make a team to upgrade the tracking system."

～

The same night at home, Karen couldn't budge from the thoughts of the video she saw. 'What site was that? Who could do that?' She wondered. Her mind kept conjuring up the logic behind men slicing women and drinking their blood but couldn't come up with any. 'Had it been true, this video would have been viral on the internet or made breaking news already,' she thought. Night fell on the Conecuh city, and the streets displayed abandonment. At home, Karen was snuck under the soft embrace of her comforter and looking at her PC. She looked over at her wall clock that read 11:45 p.m. and willed against her will to open her computer. Soon, she gave in to her urge. She swung her feet off the bed, found her slippers, and walked up to sit across from her PC. She flicked on the computer and ran her codes all over again to track and unlock all the databases.

Ten of the networks that emerged were easily unlocked except one of them that read 'the ravers.' She entered different codes to open this one but to no avail. The ravers appeared to be the strongest of all. Karen struggled to boil down her curiosity and not think of reasons why the database was so protected, but her mind kept going back to it. The idea of breaking the seal through one illegal method that she had once read in the book crossed her mind, but then her conscience shut it down. She took a complete minute to beat down her sense of morality and let the curiosity take a toll on her decision. The very next minute, she was applying the code-breaking method. It took her half an hour before unlocking the site completely.

"Welcome to Vampire Rave," said a monotone voice. Karen's excitement was over the moon upon realizing that she had opened up a vampire site. Where all the Goths on planet earth had been fathoming where Lord Byron's tribe would be, she, for one, had discovered a trail from where she could know their whereabouts. She strolled down the social media site of Vampires and explored the lives of these cold-blooded species. She tried looking up the blood-drinking and human-slicing video but couldn't find any. Cancer, together with Lazarus, had unenabled the food option from the site just in case so that the humans breeze blithely past their website, confusing it for any ordinary or hilare site on vampires.

That night, Karen discovered pretty much about the lifestyle of vampires and followed many singers, artists, sky travelers, and programmers of VampTown. The next day she went to school and couldn't wait to tell her friend, Sophia, about the site she discovered the night before. She hurried up the class and found her sitting quietly at her desk. Karen walked up to her excitedly and told her that she had to tell her something. Before that, Sophia had her face turned all red and told Karen that she had to confess something.

A while later, she informed Karen that she wasn't a Goth, the fact that she kept hidden since the beginning of school. Upon interrogation, she said that she admired Goths and particularly Karen, that was why she pretended to be one.

Karen hadn't been friends with anyone at school except Sophia; she never really thought an ordinary person would understand her. When she met Sophia for the first time, she decided to open up to her because she seemed very accepting and had the same nocturnal routine as her. Even the books she'd carry were to excite her friend, Karen so that she could inform her more about the spookiness of Goths or vampires. When Sophia made her confession and finally asked Karen about what she wanted to tell, Karen held her tongue. She left partly because she was upset with Sophia and primarily because she felt her noblest obligation toward Lord Byron's army and didn't want to get them in trouble.

For the next couple of weeks, she made a routine of delving and strolling deep into the Vampire's social networking site. She befriended many vampires who would mistake her for a vamp too but of another region. Besides her geekiness, she had one other talent of singing. To feel more like a part of their tribe, she started uploading her music videos. Soon, the videos became viral on the site and bagged her all the fame.

Not just that, she won over many vampire celebrities with her brains and wits. In no time, she became the talk of Vampire town – be it at the concert thrown in the cloud by Vampire Radio or the Vampire Rave networking site.

CHAPTER 5
INTRUDER RADAR

Vamp Town

The radar flicked on and off for weeks on end. An incredible wave of rage and haste could be observed in the demeanor of programmers, working tirelessly to shut the flicking of lights in the Vampire Rave. There was an emergency alert in the organization, and each individual felt the tension of the situation. Yet no one could feel the rising panic in the air like him. He asked the engineers to turn off the beeping because that was giving him a real rush of adrenaline. He could sense the threat all over again, just the way he did in his childhood. The memory of the battle of Trinix was still carved in his mind. Every day, while how he would watch the radar light blinking on and off, faint flashes of the war fought between the warm-blooded and cold-blooded species would hit him in waves. Upon intervals, the blood-curling image of his father's head being ripped off by the heartless human was crossing his mind. He watched the heart-wrenching visual up from the cloud shuttle where the younger him and his mother were watching the battle. He still remembered the ear-screeching screams of his mother when she watched her husband getting killed and then melting like a waxed candle, giving in to the glare of sun rays. When he had swum up out of the depth of his mind, the reality remained unchanged. He was experiencing double the burden of anxiety this time. Part of it was because the radar had been buzzing for weeks now, which meant someone had been spying on them from the earth and could track their otherwise concealed location. And the major part was his organization would have to be accountable to the officials for having such weak security settings on his website that could be tracked on earth. He and Lazarus knew the repercussions they'd have to face but more than that they dreaded the safety of the VampTown. They had sleepless days and nights, working and brainstorming a way to track the location of the spy and at the same time, tighten their security settings.

"I'm really worried now," Cancer said, pressing his thumb on his forehead. "I hope we track the intruder and confuse him about our whereabouts." He was sitting in his cabin with Lazarus, panicking about the situation. "We'll still be able to get through that in a day or two," Lazarus stated matter-of-factly, still delving into his laptop. "I'm just concerned that the officials don't find out about our poor security settings or we'll be punished to death."

"I don't care about that, Lazarus," Cancer retorted. "I don't mind being taken to jail or given scorching treatment. I just don't

want to put the life of our vampire tribe at stake again. My grandfather had saved it from the mouth of extinction, and I don't want to be the one ruining it for him and all of us." Lazarus put a gentle hand on Cancer's knees. "It's okay, my friend. You aren't ruining Lord Byron's legacy. If anything, you are polishing it with wit, empathy, and kindness towards your tribe." Cancer shook his head in disapproval while Lazarus went on. "Your grandfather must be very proud of you. Trust me."

"I hope so," Cancer said, disappointedly. Lazarus picked up his cell phone and started scrolling down his Vampire Rave account. "By the way," he attempted. "Did you go over the trending searches of our site?"

"Yeah," Cancer said, standing up and walking around to sit next to Lazarus. "1. Karen Lewis — the rising star. 2. Joseph Keith — the girl bloodsucker. 3. Dr. Jonathan — the organic blood adviser." Cancer plainly said. "But I haven't seen any of the videos yet."

"Me neither," Lazarus said. He opened up the trendiest video on the site and played it. They watched together as a girl with clear skin and black hair strum the guitar like a pro and sang, 'Zombie' by the Cranberries. Karen quite carefully thought out the way to post her video, so as not to give the slightest clue to anyone about the "Whoa." Cancer ran short of words. "She — she has a great voice, I must say."

"Hmm. Definitely," Lazarus agreed. "But what's up with her background?" He frowned.

"What?" Cancer watched closely. "It's thickly dark out there."

"It is," Lazarus responded, "but what's that?" He pointed at the small bead of the beam coming from the fairy light that was accidentally left open.

"Oh, that," Cancer quickly saw. "I don't know. A firefly maybe."

"That's exactly my question. Haven't we banned yellow lights because it causes skin blisters?" Lazarus inquired.

By the time they were trying to figure out the nature of the object, the video finished, and neither of them had the time to go over it again for that tiny shady detail. The second video they played contained the food challenge where the guy — Joseph Keith would only feed on the human girls' blood and claimed that it's yummier than that of the kid's or man's blood. In the video, he gave the details about how he attacked the girl, grazed his rodent teeth in her windpipe, and sucked the sweetest blood he could have.

"Okay," Cancer said. "But I still prefer to have deer's blood— sweet, scrumptious, and less calorie count. Moving on," he tapped the third link. "Ah, here is a typo."

In the third video, a well-dressed man was suggesting the right dietary habit and routine for the vami- teeth. Both Lazarus and Cancer watched the video till the end before Raul — the assistant manager appeared.

"Sir, our developers have tracked the proximal location using the GPS. Can you please come over to check?" Raul said to no one in particular.

Lazarus gave Cancer a look — that meant (see, I told you not to worry) and both of them paced after Raul who headed into the developer's room. A young geek boy was sitting at the corner greeted Cancer and Lazarus.

"Hello, Luther," Cancer chirped. "What's up? What did you find?" The Cancer had a friendly attitude towards all his employees. He had given them the autonomy to present their ideas and speak their mind. He had maintained a healthy flat hierarchy where every voice was heard, and

everyone was allowed to play an integral part in the success of an organization.

"All is well, sir," Luther smiled. "I've spotted the city, that is, Alabama and the closest I could get is the Conecuh forest." He zoomed in and moved his finger around the yellow round region. "This is the region where the intruder is getting the connections."

"How fat is this region?" Lazarus asked. "Sixty-seven acres," Luther said.

"Great job, boy," Cancer patted Luther on the back. He felt a sense of elation at the news. He was quite delighted over the idea that he was closer to discovering the intruder. Now the only thing he and his bunch of programmers had to work on was improving the networking and security settings. He had to find a way to slim the satellite signals so that they could only be confined to the VampTown and not extend down on earth.

"Keep it up, Luther," Lazarus said. "Keep working towards it till we get to the address of the intruder."

Cancer got up and started crooning the song he had heard Karen singing.

"Whoa. Whoa," Lazarus said. "Somebody's a fan of the firefly girl already."

Cancer looked over at his friend and realized he'd been singing her song subconsciously. If he were to say he didn't like the song or the girl for that matter, it would be incorrect. The moment he saw her, he felt a weird connection with her. The mere sight of her made him cudgel his brains. That round face, almond eyes, thick lips, and black hair. He was familiar with them but couldn't recall how. In response to Lazarus, he just smiled and trod back to his cabin.

Alabama City, September 11, 2018, Dixon Club.

The nightclub was a heartbeat on a loudspeaker. Its rainbow lights and throbbing beat revved up the soul and invited all to unite as one in the heavenly vibe. Olivia, the most athletic girl at Karen's school, was busy grooving to the beat of Sia's "Chandelier" blaring aloud with a weird mix of DJ. Just then, she felt thirsty after breaking loose for God knows how long and ambled up to the counter.

"Mineral water, please?" she asked the brunette bartender on the counter. The boy went straight for the fridge and got her one bottle. In the meantime, she sensed her phone ringing in her left denim pocket. She pulled it out and saw the recipient read, 'mama calling.'

The very next minute, she was on the lane leading to her home. Her ears were still buzzing from the music as she took her walk home from the best party ever. The party possessed all the right people, the right energy, and the right vibes. The attendees were busy grooving, laughing, gossiping, and living it up if you name it. She wouldn't have left this early if it weren't for her mom berating her badly on the phone. She just ruined her mood. Her mother knew all the right things to say to get her daughter to leave the party. One great thing about going home early was that she would have all the stamina for the marathon tomorrow. She was in the final and needed rest to win it. It was primarily due to this reason that she had quickly agreed on coming home. However, she knew it wouldn't be too hard to win the race since she was the fastest in school, yet she had thought it was the right thing to do at that time.

Parker, the boy she had been doting on since semester one, had offered her to drop home. She had refused right away. She knew if she had said yes, they'd have spent another hour or two on the road making out in the car. Taking her route home on foot, she was immediately reminded of the last time they had made out. As she was talking in the car, he listened to her silently. His eyes were interlocked continuously with hers, and before she could see it coming, he had gently put his lips on hers; pressing it softly and carefully taking in her upper and lower lips between his before their tongues met.

Olivia quickly swam up out of the depth of her nostalgia before she started craving him badly and change her decision of going home. On her way, she gave her and Parker's relationship a real thought. Parker was a socially awkward and less talkative guy who had never been observed talking to any girl except Olivia. She still remembered the very first day as he walked up the school entrance and made literal head-turns of not just girls but boys as well. Olivia happened to be pretty much a geek then and had no other focus besides her studies. She remembered looking at him as he looked back and heedlessly delved back into her book.

The not-so-little things and not-so-little moments kept occasioning since then when Parker chose Olivia as her project partner, and lunch partner and even nominated her name as his cheer girl for the interdepartmental basketball match. The envious glares and unsaid cusses were quite evident in other girls' demeanor. Olivia too wanted to escape the deadly stares but didn't know for herself why Parker was doing that until he confessed his love in the most unusual way at the very first night party.

"I love you like I loved no one before," he had mouthed amidst rhythmic panting. "I want you to love me too. Will you?"

"Oh, okay. Um. Are you proposing to me or asking me to make out with you?" Olivia had replied.

"I don't know," he had responded, straight-faced. "Just never ask me about my past." He had paused. "So, what's your answer?"

After giving it some thought, Olivia said yes. They had made out several times, but their relationship wasn't like any other couple. Parker wouldn't talk like other boyfriends do but loved her like no other. This one factor had kept her clung to him and dragged the geek like her to parties, if that would mean making love with him.

On her way home, smiling over their memories, she breezed past the Conecuh lane thick with gnarled trees. The further she walked, the more suffocating the darkness felt. She sensed an odd air infused in her surroundings. She wrinkled her brows and studied her environment.

"Something's wrong," she told herself and skidded to a halt. She looked around. No soul seemed to be present on the street except her. Shrugging her feeling off, she went on walking. She ambled past the park and heard movement. She froze. Upon looking over her shoulder, again she found no one around. She started strolling when the next moment she heard footsteps behind her. She paused. Ahead of her stood thick gnarled trees in line and overhead, the crooked branches pulled her hair against gravity. Or so she felt. On hearing the footsteps, she whipped around just in time to see a flash of movement, but that was all.

At precisely that moment, she felt the prickles swarming beneath her clothes and scalp. Panic flared up inside her as the sinister feeling gripped her unrehearsed. She broke into a run immediately, her heart steadily thudding as she did. She fought the winds and maintained her pace regardless. Hardly three minutes later, she slowed down when nothing much happened. She gave her forehead a slight tap over her folly just then she heard a chuckle from behind her. Her hands started shaking badly, and her heart bludgeoned in her chest. She spun around and saw an evil creature grinning at her. He had jet black hair, pale, blood-soaked skin, a pointed nose, blood-red eyes, tall structure. He was wearing a black shirt with shiny black jeans.

"You shouldn't have stopped sprinting," he sarcastically said, lolling his tongue to one side. He eyed her up and down, wearing a short denim skirt and baggy white top. Olivia could read through his malicious appeal. She took small careful steps back and whirled around in the other direction. Working up her athletic muscles, she paced as fast as she could. Breaking cold sweat, she kept looking over her shoulder to see if the apparition was following, but she could see nothing except an orangish gush of wind falling in and out of sight. She kept on racing for a bit, then as she thought she had left him behind, there he stood, some meters ahead of her.

She trained her feet to the left and paced through the suffocating darkness of the park. She camouflaged herself in the shade of gnarled trees with crooked branches. She looked through the slits of the leaves, and he wasn't there. Gone. Maybe. A snake slithered past her and immediately after a black cat crossed her way. She saw her fingertips turning pale and blue out of fear. Suddenly, an ice-cold hand gripped her shoulder and slammed her against the trunk of the tree. A stinging pain ran over Olivia's nose as the blood dripped everywhere. Regardless of the ache, she spun around to see the apparition and observed the hungry glint in his eyes.

"Please, don't kill me," Olivia pleaded. "Please let me go."

His expressions remained just the same. He advanced

toward her and opened his mouth to reveal sharp, rodent fangs. Olivia gasped. Before she could react, the creature grabbed her hair, pulled her close, and dug his face into her neck. Olivia could now hear a piercing rattle in her head. The creature leaned in, and her sharp fangs pressed into her neck. She felt the excruciating pain to the point where everything blurred out, and she passed out.

The next day Karen went to school. She saw everyone giving a warm pat on Parker's shoulder, who was as expressionless as before. Karen thought for a bit about what could have happened. Just then, her friend Sophia emerged out of nowhere and gave Karen a gentle tap on the back.

"Hey," she said, as enthusiastically as always.

"Hello," Karen replied, disappointment apparent in her tone.

"Did you hear Olivia's story?" Sophia gossiped.

"Nope," Karen said curtly. "What is she saying?" She tried to hide her anger.

"Lol." Sophia chuckled. "What will she say? She's kidnapped, duh."

"What? When?" Karen shocked herself.

"Her friends say the last time they saw her at the party last night. Her parents filed a report against Parker thinking that he is behind the kidnapping," Sophia said, matter-of-factly.

"Jeez! Why would he do that? He's been his boyfriend since forever," Karen snorted.

"Thanks for stating the obvious, honey," Sophia remarked. "But he's the weirdest kind in our school. He's the easiest suspect. And truth be told, I always get criminal vibes from him if I ignore his dashing looks."

"Well, I don't think so," Karen defended. "Ignore the quirks; everyone is different. He sure does love her. I can see that." Karen looked over at him. Parker's social awkwardness was apparent from the way he was dealing with the parts of people. He was already depressed, and the students' sympathy was worsening things for him.

"Can't you see the way he's behaving?" Sophia said. She cast an annoying glance at him, which he caught, stood up, and left. "Such a weirdo."

Karen looked over at him till he diffused out of sight. "Did the police visit his place?"

"Not sure about his place, but they came here twenty minutes before you dropped in. Inquired him and left," Sophia said. She pulled out the chips of Doritos and continued, "Boy was taken aback by the news. That I agree but still don't know how much of it was pretense and how much of it was genuine. He stated that he did offer to drop her home, but she refused. Since there is no evidence against him, the police left without another word."

"Poor guy," Karen pitied. She started walking up the stairs for the first lesson of the day. Sophia followed. Karen wanted to ignore Sophia. Not that her love for her friend had alleviated upon discovering that she wasn't Goth but for the fact that she felt deception. No matter how hard she tried to forget about it, she wasn't comfortable with the idea that their relationship started on the foundation of a lie. She couldn't shake off the suspicion whether her friend had been loyal to her all these years or that she had been secretly telling her boyfriend, Carl about it. Had it been any other detail Sophia had lied about, she wouldn't have minded but the fact that the spreading of this information could mean life and death for her and Laura, she felt the backstab. Sophia was unaware of the repercussions of her lie.

"Hey," Sophia cheerfully said. "It's **PHP** period.

What have you decided?"

"Decided about what?" Karen retorted.

"The project we were doing?" Sophia reminded her.

Karen deliberately gave her a clueless look. "Duh. About constructing the app that will track and connect all the databases nearby without having to enter the wifi password? Come on."

"Oh yeah," Karen simply said. She wasn't showing any interest in the conversation. Partly because she was upset with her and secondly, she dreaded unraveling the details about the vampire website she had bumped into. As a Goth herself, she felt her noblest obligation to protect their identity and hide their existence.

"How many databases have you spotted? Any information about the weird site we saw the other day?" Sophia excitedly asked.

Karen could see the dilated pupil of her friend. "As many as I did the same day you were at my place. Nothing about the spooky website. It must be a troll or something."

"It didn't look like a troll of some sort," Sophia said. She sensed the coldness in her friend's tone. "Hey, are you still upset with me about leaving your place that way?"

Karen rolled her eyes. "Jeez. No," she refused annoyingly.

"Hey," Sophia said, holding her friend's hand. "I'm sorry. I promise I'll come over again and this time I'll look for the spooky network with you. I won't get scared or leave until we're done exploring the site, I promise. Imagine how interesting our project will become."

"It's okay, Sophie," Karen said, without meeting her friend's eye. "I think we're fine without connecting with unnerving networks. What we've found is more than enough to win the project, I guess."

"But imagine Karen. With that spooky site we can't just win the project but can also make it to news channels, Guinness World Record, or even NASA," Sophia wondered.

"Oh, come on," Karen poked the dream bubble of her friend. "Let's stay where we are. Don't dream beyond our capacity."

"Okay," Sophia said, tired of making amends with Karen.

In the PHP period, Miss Angeline walked around the desk to check the students' projects and simultaneously approved and disapproved some of them. As for Karen and Sophia's project, she approved it.

"Good job," she said. "But let me tell you something. If you guys discovered any private network and its branch sites that hadn't been found before, then you may not only win the project but can also present your idea on a global platform. Have you bumped into any such network yet?"

"Yes, ma'am," Sophia immediately said. "There was this blood —"

"Nothing really," Karen interjected. "We'll let you know if we do, Miss Angelina."

"Great then," Miss Angelina smiled. "Let me know if you do. I'll help you out." She walked onto another desk.

Sophia gave her friend a suspicious look. "Why didn't you let me tell her?" she asked.

"Because we aren't sure about anything. It could be spam content that we bumped into," Karen lied.

"So what?" Sophia argued. "We could've at least discussed that with her."

"Not that important," Karen said curtly.

Sophia started suspecting her friend's behavior. She was sure either Karen had found something and is too upset to share it with her or that she had run across something troublesome and not sought her help. Either way, she was confident that Karen had found something she chose not to speak about and decided to find it out herself by paying a surprise visit to her place.

Karen went home exhausted. She was having the most depressive days of her life. At the start of it she was quite interested in the site and also made new vampire friends but all of a sudden loneliness took a toll on her. She felt alone with her friend. Her only friend, Sophia, who claimed to be a Goth; with whom Karen used to discuss everything turned out to be a human. She had no one to share her feelings with. Laura was getting old, and most of the time she wouldn't make sense of what she was saying though she tried doing that with a sweet boy, Zobray, who happened to be a tour guide of VampTown. He gave her the nitty-gritty of the VampTown and kept her hooked with the fantastic details. Zobray was a great listener. Part of it was accredited to his profession, but the other half was due to his exceptional ability to understand and solve problems.

Karen decided to open up to him because of his genuine care and concern, but due to the fear of being found, she kept her life and identity confidential. She continually fought the urge to break free from her routine and set out on an adventure, a tour. Her mind yearned for oxygen and wanted to explore places in person, but the hefty expenses involved in the process would let her do so. Exhausted from her life, routine, and loneliness, she relied on the Vampire Rave again to lend a sense of calm to her chaos. She opened it up, scrolled up and down for a while, and then picked up her guitar. She turned the camera on, closed her eyes, and sang the song Laura used to sing to her when she was a child. The next minute she uploaded it to her account.

The views exceeded to thousand in an hour and one lakh in a day. Many singers, artists, painters, and bloggers including Zobray commented on and shared her video. Soon, another video by her became viral and topped the list of trends.

~

Vamp Town

The radar had been twitching for three weeks now, and the closest the engineers had gotten to identify the intruder's location is eight acres. The situation was still panicky in the Vampire Rave. To keep his head cool, Lazarus was watching movies in every hour break he would get. Other workers had their headphones on, listening to their favorite songs to reduce the tension in the air. Meanwhile, for Cancer, the only voice lending solace to his restless soul was the voice of Karen. He had finally started following her on the social site to stay updated with her new songs. He opened the television and flicked it to the news channel. Just then, the news of Karen emerged on the screen.

"News Alert: Vampire priests are considering Karen, the revolutionary voice that Lord Byron had given insights about."

Interviewer: Yes, Priest Cassius. What do you think about this girl – Karen's voice?

Priest: Years ago, Lord Byron wrote in his scripture that a melodious voice would emerge out of the blue and make everyone groove over her beat. This voice will either forge an apocalypse or revolution in the vampire world. I think the voice has finally reached our region and it's time for all the vampires to brace themselves.

Interviewer: How can you say it's the same voice?

Priest: Dear. I assure you it's this girl, Karen. Cause I heard her singing a song in Czech in her latest video and that was the language only Lord Byron or his grandson, Cancer is familiar with. Czech is a language Lord Byron would communicate in with me to conceal the message from the enemy. Now the question arises how does this girl know the language? You must call her here and ask where did she hear this.

Cancer quickly turned the TV off and opened up his PC. He went over his data facts and soon saw the name of Karen's new song on the top list of Trendies. He clicked the link and Karen appeared in the same nightwear and the same blackout in the background. In no time, she started singing a song in Czech which his grandfather, Lord Byron, used to sing for him. Cancer scratched his head, wondering how and where did she hear this from. He went back and opened her profile. He looked for her address that said VampTown. He ran the link, but nothing appeared. Soon Cancer realized that the address was deceptively made. Just then, Raul appeared.

"Sir?" he happily said. "Luther has found the location of the intruder."

Cancer immediately stood up and followed Raul to the developers' room. Sitting in the corner, Luther was busy on the computer. Just when he observed Cancer coming, he gave him a reassuring nod. Soon, Luther zoomed in on the location of the stalker which read, Conecuh, street 1, James and Bella's territory.

"Okay," Cancer panted. "That was accurate. Can you please see the user name of the stalker for me, Luther?"

"Sure thing," Luther said. He quickly looked up the details using computer codes and stated, "Here it is, sir."

Cancer leaned in and couldn't believe himself as he read, "Karen Lewis." Immediately after reading the name, he was immediately taken back to the time when he was sitting in the cloud shuttle with his mother and vampires were losing it in the battle of Trinix. Every living vampire made it to the cloud shuttle except a few Goths. Lord Byron came rushing for the cloud shuttle when he realized that an old Goth lady and her granddaughter had been left in the tent. He immediately trudged out of the shuttle and went to get them. In no time, he brought along with him the same old lady and her infant granddaughter. On reaching the cloud shuttle, the old lady was losing it. She cried, whined, and mourned the death of her son and daughter-in-law. Upon hearing her shrieks, the infant baby also started crying. Watching the situation get out of hand, Lord Byron sang a Czech song that made the baby go silent immediately. The old lady, who also had been weeping aloud, seemed to get her senses back.

Down on earth, Karen was blithely strolling down the Vampire Rave when suddenly she lost the networks of the website. Surprised herself, she leaned in and entered the codes, but nothing worked. Soon, her PC got hanged, and the next minute a face appeared on the screen.

"Hello, Karen," the man smiled. "You might not have an idea who I am, but I know who you are."

"Hey," Karen replied nervously. "Um. May I know who I am talking to?"

"Yes," he replied. "It's Cancer Byron – the grand- son of Lord Byron and founder of Vampire Rave."

Karen froze in her spot. "Don't worry, Karen," he continued. "We know you have been stalking our system for some time now and trying to blend in."

"I'm – I'm sorry," Karen apologized. "Please forgive me."

"Chill out, Karen," Cancer softly said. "We have found that you're a Gothic descendant yourself. We intend no harm either."

"Oh," Karen was speechless.

"Instead, we owe the Gothics our lives for how they sacrificed themselves during the Battle of Trinix and proved their loyalty. Your parents, James, and Bella Lewis have also fought like warriors without caring about their infant daughter." He paused, wiped a tear, and then stated. "For this reason, we've decided to pay back. Therefore, we've decided to invite you over to our world to stay forever. Would you like to come?"

Karen didn't know what to say. She took a while before answering, "I live with my grandmother, Laura." She swallowed down hard. "I can't leave her alone like this."

"Okay, if that's the case. Will you be our guest for some days? We'll give you a good tour of our place and greet you like our very own people." He cleared his throat and continued. "Also, your voice is becoming the new anthem for parties, tours, and concerts. We are also calling you over for having a concert. Our people are dying to groove to your songs live."

Cancer took her in confidence with all the details of Gothics and Vampire's familiarity and brotherhood. So, she hardly took much time before saying yes.

The next day Cancer came on air with two big news. The first is about the new features concerning the security settings of vampires' social media accounts and the second is about the arrival of Karen in VampTown. He didn't reveal how he approached Karen and kept her identity a secret. The vampires thought that she belonged to another VampTown and started preparing for her welcome oblivious to her blood type.

CHAPTER 6
FRESHLY MINCED GIRLS

Karen sat motionless in her room, staring at the computer screen. It had been long since Cancer ebbed and dwindled to nothing, leaving the computer screen and the system hanged. Outside, the midnight scattered progressively across the night sky, projecting a blend of inky and pitch-black down at the city.

The winds hitting Karen's window were colder and damper than they had been. Every ten seconds, her eyes would fall on the curtains swaying over the beat of the winds and back at the infinite rain-washed darkness beyond the window, but would soon return to the computer screen on which Cancer appeared two hours ago. She couldn't recover from the shock of being approached and invited by Cancer Byron – the grandson of Lord Byron, to his town - The Vampires town. She couldn't quite grasp the reality of the situation.

The decision she made in front of him to visit his town was somewhat taken hastily. She didn't want to turn up to be a disappointment to Lord Byron's grandson, who took the time to invite her over as the guest of honor in his town. Moreover, it had been her dream to sing for a bigger crowd, and she couldn't see a better opportunity than this. Besides, in the first five seconds of watching him turn the screen on, she developed a growing admiration and sense of respect toward him. She even felt a soothing connection with him that she hadn't felt towards anyone in ages. Cancer's invitation seemed so genuine and considerate that she knew she could trust him.

She swam up out of the depths of her thoughts and looked over at the clock that read, 4:04 a.m. On the other end of the window, the darkness of the night sky was diluting, giving in to the approaching twilight. She had school in the morning, and sleep was necessary, but her mind kept conjuring up thoughts, prompting her to execute. And so, she did. She pushed her duvet, swung her legs off the bed, and walked around her bed to reach the computer. Her PC was still on, and the yellow light under the power button of the CPU was still blinking. She grabbed the chair across from it and sat down. With the shake of the mouse, the desktop came to life.

She kept herself busy on the computer till the dawn broke. Soon the sunlight streamed across her floor like a golden brook, and she turned to look at it. Instead of tremors, the sunlight filled her with gratitude. She breathed a sigh of relief since she was done with her task. Up above the window wall, the clock struck eight, reminding her of school. She got up and headed for the bathroom. In the next fifteen minutes, she was done bathing, ironing her clothes, eating her breakfast, and ready for school.

Vamp Town

Ever since Cancer had announced Karen's arrival, the news channels couldn't stop talking about her overnight success. The three other hashtags to top the trending list of every social media platform were: #TheMuchAwaitedConcert, #Karen-TheCzechEnigma, and #TheArrivalOfAMelodyQueen. Despite that, none of them could guess the details of her whereabouts. They discussed how Cancer would've tracked the hidden gem of the Vamp Town through his extensive database and would soon exhaust the topic. Most of their concern was centric on her melodious voice and the preparations that were being done for her arrival.

Cancer, on the other hand, was quite happy about discovering the girl he shared some of his childhood memories with. He remembered how, and when the cloud shuttle landed in the VampTown, no one could console little Karen except his grandfather. Lord Byron had equal concerns for the baby girl who just lost her parents in the battle and had no mother to feed her. On those days, he would fetch goat milk from Earth to suffice little Karen's hunger.

Laura was too disturbed psychologically over the loss of her son and daughter-in-law that she could hardly return from her daze state to check in on her granddaughter. It went on for a couple of weeks before both the Gothic families began finding it hard to live in the VampTown. The first problem with living in their world was the bone-chilling cold and no presence of sun at all. The colder the weather would get, the more it would prompt their hunger. And hunger wouldn't have been a problem in an otherwise scenario, but VampTown was located in a far-fetched cloud, and the possibility of having fertile land and yielding crops was out of the question.

Soon the three Gothic families, including Laura and her granddaughter, were running wild out of hunger and cold. Perhaps, the winter was augmenting their grief of losing their loved ones in the battle. So, with a very heavy heart, Cancer decided to send the Gothics on Earth for their betterment stealthily. Another concern that was eating Byron alive was the safety of the Gothics, who could easily be spotted by the humans living in Phoenix town. So, he used his magic and speculated the densely populated region of humans. He told the Goth families what he was up to and used his most complicated spell to wipe out the memory of the battle from the minds of the residents living in that area.

Once he was done with that, he forged three houses at an alternative distance using his magic. At that point, he transported the Gothics to Earth with a promise that they'll be remembered for their sacrifices and loyalty. He further pledged to protect them and be readily available in their times of need. That was the first and last time Cancer saw his grandfather's teary eyes, not because he had to bid the Gothics goodbye, but due to the close bond that he shared with the baby in that short period.

He remembered how, once as a kid, when he was busy playing with little Karen whom he adored, he heard his grandfather talking to Priest Cassius about the baby.

"How is the baby getting along?" Priest Cassius enquired, looking at the baby in the metallic bassinet.

Lord Byron followed his gaze and looked over at the baby Karen, who was busy cooing and playing with four-year-old Cancer. "Oh, pretty well. Thank goodness," he replied.

"Finally," Priest Cassius sighed. "I was concerned about how the baby would do after her mother's death. Too early for her to even spot the changes around her."

"I know," Lord Byron stated, looking down at his feet. "You know, Cassius," he paused and tried to conjure up his thoughts.

"I haven't loved a baby as much as I loved this little girl. In the past few weeks, I haven't once thought that she was any different from us. Though she holds sweet blood, but never did I once feel inclined towards tasting it," he lost deep in thought and then continued. "I cannot believe how she treats me like family though she's hardly a month or two old."

Priest Cassius smiled. "Babies are like that. Their adorableness and quirky retorts make you forget the world. We're blessed to have the baby that is a source of our Lord's happiness and joy," he bowed.

Lord Byron beamed at Cassius's generosity and continued. "I feel no guilt in telling you that I never felt this connection with Alaric and Blade as well. This baby is different. I love her till no end. And everything I've loved has either brought about an apocalypse or revolution. Irina instigated the battle; I expect the opposite from this one." Just then, the baby girl started whining, and Lord Byron rose and marched across to comfort her. "I'll speak with you later, Cassius," he said and disappeared into the room where Cancer had taken her.

A couple of weeks later, when they had to say goodbye to the baby for her good, Cancer couldn't keep it together. Even hours after she was gone, he couldn't stop sobbing and wailing. Upon looking at his condition, Lord Byron took his grandson to his study room.

"Dear," Lord softly said. "I need to show you something." He pulled out his golden scripture of predictions and flipped to page 87 for Cancer to read.

I say this with so much faith about the time when I won't be around. But you all — the coming generation — will be there. It is when the revolution will come. For if you remain patient and steadfast, you'll see it and get the best of it. And if you don't, then you must presume the end is looming near for the vampirism. This revolution wouldn't be a consequence of global issues or planetary movements. Here, I am talking about the emergence of a Gothic enigma, a girl, who will bridge the gap between the vampires and Goths and unite them as one. And I must tell you that you must unite because she will appear at the time when the vampirism would be on the verge of becoming extinct.

I must as well inform you to fight the urge to devour her blood. Make sure you don't bring out the best in her because the apocalypse resides in her wrath. Her rage could be the end of vampirism. It isn't to say; you shouldn't seek her out at all. As a matter of fact, you must do that just in time to maintain your stealth and not encounter another war outbreak. Therefore, when she appears, handle her with care because I've given her the secret to unraveling the holy verse of the second scripture.

In the next twenty minutes, Karen was in school. Her behavior had haste that she wasn't familiar with. The class of **PHP** was due in five minutes, so she hurried to the cafeteria and grabbed Sophia by the hand.

"Whoa. What?" Sophia was surprised to see the urgency of her friend.

"I need to show you something," Karen said.

Sophia immediately got up and followed her friend to the visuals and computer lab. "What is it, Karen?" she inquired. "Have you found something fishy again?"

"Again?" Karen picked the word. "What do you mean by 'again'?"

"Uh, I meant the spooky content we found the other day? Remember?" Sophia pressed.

"What nonsense?" Karen burst out. "I told you it was nothing but an illusion. You better focus on what's important!" she complained.

"Okay," Sophia raised her hands in defense. "Relax now."

Karen felt a pang of guilt washing over her. She gave her head a disapproving shake and apologized. "Look. I'm sorry," she mouthed. "I'm just in a hurry." She retrieved her USB from the pocket and plugged it into one of the systems. She selected one of the folders that had the initials of Karen and Sophia (KS) and clicked it open. Hardly a second or two later, a wide range of databases emerged on the screen.

"Why are you in such a hurry, Karen?" Sophia studied the behavior of her friend closely. "We have another week for this."

"I know," Karen replied with a sigh. "But I won't be around from tomorrow onwards."

"Won't be around?" Sophia squinted. "What do you mean? Are you going somewhere?"

Karen ignored her questions and showed her the links to databases. "Here," she pointed, "is a list of all the networks I could track. And I'm sure these are all. There is no point in delaying it. So," she cleared her throat, "it would be better if we submit this to Miss Angelina."

Sophia rolled her eyes. "Okay, let me check." She was pissed by her friend's behavior now. "Karen," she said, pointing at the screen, "pick any of the uncanny networks that Miss Angelina was talking about."

"Different, you mean?" Karen queried. "Yeah. Well, this network you see right here belongs to criminals," she pointed at one of the links at the bottom. "And this one," she scrolled up and pressed one of the longest backlinks, "is a big database of cybercriminals."

"And?" Sophia asked curiously.

"And what?" Karen retorted. "This is more than enough for us to win the project."

"See," Sophia tried to explain. "I'm not only thinking about winning the school project. I just want this to be the national platform caliber."

"It is already, my friend," Karen replied. "I worked overnight on this to release your burden while I'm away, all for you to possess such disbelief." She behaved offensively.

"No, Karen," Sophia defended. "I love it. I appreciate the networks you've come up with. I'm just saying if we get more time, maybe we can find something."

"Well," Karen plainly said. "That was all from my end. And we'll ask Miss Angelina about this. If she likes it so far, then I don't think we should go walk the extra mile to deliver the project."

With that, Karen and Sophia returned to the classroom where students were greeting Miss Angelina.

"Morning students," she softly greeted back. "I hope you all had a great weekend."

"Not really," half the class crooned.

"Super busy," the other half chanted.

"I see," Miss Angelina turned to look at Karen and Sophia, slowly waking into the classroom. "Oh, hello, girls. Get to your seats." Karen and Sophia nodded the greetings at her over which she gleamed and secured their place next to each other.

"Okay. So, how far are you all with the projects?" she piped. "Raise your hands in case of any concern."

Karen shot her hand up in the air and, without forethought, said, "We're done with our project!"

"Whoa," Miss Angelina exclaimed. "That's very fast. Plus five marks for the early submissions."

Sophia looked over at Karen in shock. She had her jaw dropped for a bit, and then, as if retrieving from the shock, she said, "What are you saying, Karen? We're supposed to ask her first." Karen ignored Sophia. She looked away from her friend and told Miss Angelina, "Ma'am, we would like you to have a look at it first."

"Okay," Miss Angelina excitedly strolled towards their desks and asked for the brief.

"Miss Angelina," Sophia said. "For now, we have our project ready on the USB. If your mind has a look, we can proceed with it if necessary."

"Well. Well. Girls!" Miss Angelina energetically said. "I trust the work of you two. I've already given you five marks, so there is no getting away with it. Still, if you want me to check, come on over to the computer lab after class as I go over your project."

"Thanks a lot, Miss Angelina," Karen smiled. She felt a burden off her chest and enjoyed the rest of the lecture, while Sophia was badly pissed at her. She couldn't understand why Karen was doing this. She didn't think lying about her Gothic culture deserved as big a punishment to put up with such behavior from her friend. More than that, she regretted making her confession to Karen at all about her non-Gothic identity. The time in the class was frozen. She couldn't wait for Miss Angelina to have a look at the links so as for her to point out blunders in them. Her ferocity started taking a toll on her, and now she was willing to do anything to stop the project submission.

Soon the bell rang, and she abruptly stood up and followed Miss Angelina. Karen watched her friend's demeanor and followed her too. Sophia stopped Miss Angelina outside the lecture hall to have a conversation.

"Miss Angelina," she said. "May I have a word with you?"

"Yes, dear," the teacher intoned and watched as Karen joined the two of them in the conversation. Upon recalling her folly, she lightly snapped at her head and said, "Oh, thank you, girls. Such devoted students you are," she chuckled. "I almost forgot that I had to check the USB," she geared her feet across the narrow corridor leading to the computer lab. In hardly a minute, the three of them were inside. Miss Angelina went over all the links and looked extremely impressed with the criminals and cyber-crime networks, which she would've otherwise ignored if Karen hadn't spoken at length about the process she underwent to track and unlock these databases.

Sophia tried her best to ask for more time and emphasized how incomplete the project seemed, but Miss Angelina insisted that their early delivery would encourage others to be quick with their deliveries too. With that, the two friends left the lab and went their different ways. Karen didn't have the energy to give explanations to her friend about why she did what she did. And Sophia was extremely annoyed and decided to never speak with her friend until she'd approached her with explanations.

~

10:00 p.m. - Alabama City

Karen was in her room, as usual. She couldn't work up the nerve to run her codes and open up the Vampire Rave site. She kept staring at the blank screen of her computer and wondered whether it would be right on her part to visit the VampTown without informing anyone. Deep down inside, she was sure that she could trust Cancer but couldn't expect the same welcome from the other vampires. And rightly so, the video she saw on their social site could instill doubts and fear in anyone.

Besides, what would she tell her granny where she was going? Suddenly, she wasn't too sure if she'd be able to make it to the VampTown. She felt a gush of anxiety, doubt, and distress all of a sudden and didn't know how to escape it. She had decided not to open up the site now when it had come to their notice how she'd been intruding on it.

When it all started hitting her in waves, she decided to break free from the confinement of her room and went to the living room. Perched in the corner, Laura was sitting in her rocking chair and watching TV. Karen strolled up to the living room and secured her place on the couch, sitting opposite the TV set. An old show, Pink Panther, was running on the television, which – her granny had told her multiple times – was her father's favorite cartoon. Karen gazed at her granny's face out of warmth. The wrinkles, the freckles, the blemishes, and some scars from the battle; all glowed in the fluorescent light. Karen couldn't fight the urge to hug her granny tightly, so she walked around the couch and took her granny in an embrace.

"Oh dear," Laura gasped out of surprise. She was a little shaky in the first five seconds, but then she wrapped her arms around her granddaughter. They remained in the same position for a minute or two before Karen released her thinking about the weight she was putting on her weak granny. She sat down on the couch again and wiped the tears off her face.

"What happened, honey?" Laura asked in her frail voice.

"Nothing much," Karen mumbled. "Just missing mom and dad."

"Oh, love," Laura reached for her granddaughter's hand and grasped it softly. "Let me tell you the love story of your parents," she said.

"Granny?" Karen interrupted. "Can you tell me where VampTown is?"

Laura looked over at her granddaughter excitedly, and her eyes sparkled like they never did before. "Oh my God, Karen," she exclaimed. "How did you come to know about this town?"

"Uh," Karen went speechless for a second but quickly covered it by saying, "You've mentioned it, granny. Many times."

"Have I?" Laura scratched her head but soon exhausted the question. "Perhaps, I'm becoming very forgetful these days. What about it, dear? What do you wanna know?"

"Just – everything about it," Karen contemplated the queries she had in her mind and spoke, "Where is it located? What kind of carnivores are they? How did they get along with Goths, who had as sweet blood as any human? Their lifestyle? Eating habits? Basically, everything."

"Okay," Laura mentally memorized all the questions before answering each. "Much that I recall, VampTown is a far-fetched cloud. And it was no ordinary dewy puff of cloud. This was a real bone-chilling one. The cloud shuttle mounted up the dull region of clouds and landed some feet beneath the planets."

Karen had her eyes bawling out of her sockets. Part of it was due to the excitement, and the other half was due to the adrenaline rush.

"And for their appetite," Laura continued. "They do suck humans' blood but not Gothics. I'm not precisely sure about the reason. It could either be the oath they took on the command of Lord Byron to consider us their brothers/sisters or our nocturnal routine that makes our blood sour. Not too sure about it," she shrugged.

"Okay, got it," Karen said. "And?"

"And they got along with us well. They didn't exhibit any kind of contempt or malevolent intent. Or at least none that I could've sensed. And you, my girl, were Lord Byron's favorite child," She gently stroked her hand over Karen's face. "Back then, I had completely lost it over the loss of my son and daughter-in-law, but they took special care of you."

Karen smiled. Suddenly she found herself making up her mind to pay a visit to a place where she was loved this much. And that too by Lord Byron himself.

"They have the same routine as us," Laura continued. "Sleep in the morning, stay up at night, and party. And they'd feed on the," she tried to cudgel her brains. "I'm sorry for the glitches, dear. I wasn't in my senses during those days. But I remember Lord Byron had once preached to them all to go for deer's blood since it was the most organic and healthy blood for their tribe."

"Got it completely," Karen said enthusiastically. "Your stay would've been otherwise amazing if it weren't for the loss of mom and dad."

"Uh, not real —"

"I know," Karen interjected. "You just can't stop talking about it. I'm sure you love it. And by the way, granny, I'm going for a tour to —" She paused and came up with a name, "Huntsville. For ten days. I'll be back soon. You got to take care of yourself."

"Oh," Laura sounded concerned. "When are you leaving, dear? Who else is accompanying you?"

"Have a 5:00 a.m. flight tonight. Will leave at around 4:00 a.m.," Karen informed. "And I applied for the trip through a site. I may not be familiar with the people I'll be surrounded by, but I trust the organization that is arranging the trip. So, it'll be fine." Karen smiled.

"Okay, dear," Laura replied as a wave of relief washed over her. "I'll be awake. Reach out to me if you need any help.

"Sure, granny," Karen said, beaming at Laura, and went to her room.

By around 4:00 a.m., she was done packing her clothes and bits of snacks and dry fruits. She wasn't sure if she was going to get the right food there, so she made the arrangements accordingly. The next minute she was out of her room, dragging her bag across the living room where Laura was still busy watching Pink Panther.

She marched forth and called out, "Granny? I'm leaving."

Laura left her weaving aside, walked towards her granddaughter, and embraced her. "Take care, my love. You're all I have."

"I will, granny. Don't worry. I'll be back soon."

With that, she headed for the door and recalled the instructions of Cancer Byron.

"Please, if possible. Try to teach the Conecuh Forest at around 4:00 a.m. We'll try not to make you wait for long, but we can't receive you from home because of safety reasons. At around 4:15 a.m., you'll see a smoky ring on the edge of the forest. You just have to walk into it to enter our world. Don't take much longer; it'll vanish in three minutes." Karen, together with her wheeling bag, hurried toward the forest and reached just in time to climb the smoky ring and escaped the ground.

~

Vamp Town

Everything was ready. The venue set for Karen's welcome was the biggest open clubhouse in town. The music that was blaring over the speakers was as loud as thunder. The cutlery and tabletops were rattling over the vibrations, while the neon lights flashed everywhere like police sirens but were a lot more colorful. Inside the club, the Northern lights danced beneath the foggy smoke swirled with an array of blues, acid greens, hot pink, and gold. The party was going on in full swing, and the celebration went on into the night. The music blaring out loud infused with the bodies, making vampires forget how to stand still.

Zobray – Karen's internet friend – was grooving like his limbs were made out of spaghetti, while Cancer's face was a picture of pure excitement. Lazarus had his eyes affixed on his friend, Cancer, and he could tell there was no one in the house as happy about young Karen's arrival as him.

"Cancer?" Lazarus almost screamed over the loud music. "My happiest buddy. When is the girl coming over?"

"Ha-ha," Cancer laughed. "Aren't we all happy?

And she has climbed the foggy ring."

"Great," Lazarus exclaimed. "Then, we can expect her here within five minutes."

"Yes!" Cancer said. "I think we can go outside to receive her," he was already walking before he completed his sentence.

"I think you're right," Lazarus followed. He stopped at the entrance door, "But I think you should receive her."

"Oh no," Cancer negated. "You'll have to come with me."

"Not a chance, my friend. She must be nervous, stepping into our world for the first time. You invited her over and the fact she trusts you the most, so it has to be you receiving her," Lazarus explained.

"Buddy," Cancer softly said. "You're my man."

"Ha-ha," Lazarus laughed. "You go stand beside the foggy ring

We're expecting her any second now. Signal me when she's here. I'll go inside and prep the crowd."

"Okay, I will," Cancer acknowledged.

Though it took Karen a complete five minutes to reach VampTown, for her, it happened in the blink of an eye. She felt like she'd been sucked in with the pull of a magnet and thrown into the streets of VampTown where night prevailed. In beholding a diaphanous and snowy dress, she felt herself feeling like a shiny cloud in the thick, velvety darkness. She didn't want to wear a transparent dress, revealing her skin, but down at the earth, the weather was too hot. The gown she wore was long and thin, but not see-through. However, the same gown made her feel at home, the ease she hadn't otherwise felt on earth wearing her black collection.

Five minutes in the foggy ring and she felt a sudden push that shoved her out of the hazy transport and threw her into the arms of Cancer. The grandson of Lord Byron immediately grabbed her.

"Are you okay?" he mouthed out of concern.

Karen immediately looked up at Cancer and recognized him from the video call. She brought herself to her feet and quickly said, "I'm fine."

Lazarus watched the entire scene and giggled under his breath. He knew Cancer would've been too mesmerized to see Karen that he forgot to signal him to prepare the vamp-tooth for the surprise party. So, he went inside to silence the music, leaving the two alone in the dark.

"I hope you didn't undergo much trouble to make it here for us," Cancer asked curiously.

"Umm. Not really," Karen allowed the words to come out. "Thanks for having me over. I'm honored."

"Pleasure having you here, Karen." Cancer couldn't stop smiling. "Would you mind coming inside? Your fans can't wait to see you and hear you sing."

"Sure," Karen said.

Cancer led the way. He softly pushed the door open, got her in, entered himself, and closed the door behind him. Karen could hear her heart thudding in her chest in the silence and darkness that befell the nightclub. She waited for someone to turn on the lights and cursed herself for not being prepared for the darkness that was sure to loom in the vampire world. Then, much to her relief, a red light flicked on, but only on the empty stage located in the west. In no time, she saw a huge machine that looked like a mincer being pushed onto the stage.

The next minute two dizzy girls were brought on stage by a tall man wearing a black cloak. What he did next swept the earth beneath Karen's feet. He threw the body of one of the girls into what looked like a meat mincing machine and collected her remains in a big tray.

Fear gripped Karen, and cold shivers ran down her spine. Meanwhile, she heard the roars of the joy of the other vampires present in the same hall and felt their feet thudding on the same ground around her. Even without looking, she could tell their smiles were extended toward her in an attempt to get her attention to themselves. Their bodies swooned together as they celebrated the grinding of two innocent girls. Karen felt a tickle in her belly, and coldness made her stiff in her position. She looked up again at the stage and saw the fresh outpour of the blood being collected in a Tibetan metal chanting bowl.

Sensing a soft touch on her shoulder, she immediately whisked it away, constantly thinking about what had she gotten herself into. She felt the pull of the hand again but impulsively kicked it away. All this time, she couldn't help but wonder what if the welcome was this ugly, what the stay would be like.

And the very next minute, the lights flicked on.

CHAPTER 7
KAREN –THE SWEETEST COOKIE

4:17 a.m., Alabama City, Conecuh forest

At around twilight, the scenic salmon and purple sky were only beginning to replace the vast expanse of a jet-black night. The curtain of the surrendering night was still drawn across the vast ocean of luminous stars. Some were dull, flickering on and off at intervals as if unaware of the approaching dawn, whereas the rest were shimmering confidently in the moonless sky as if their reign was forever to stay. The forest of Conecuh was thick with trees, and yet Sam saw what he shouldn't have seen. The bare branches of the tall trees spiked into the sky with no sign of any other being in the woods. Sam, who was half-drunk and half-sober, couldn't tell if what he saw had any element of truth in it.

He was an active member of the Music Society and shared his loyalty with Peter. Weeks ago, at Dixon's club, he played an active role in ruining the Entertainment Society's Halloween party. Now it was their turn to throw the grand ghost-themed party and have a multitude of students over for the fun and spooky disco night. To their disappointment, hardly a few people visited their party, and that too out of Peter's fear, while the rest stayed back home. Peter sensed it. He knew that this time around, students weren't going to show up. Part of it was because of the disappearing episodes of girls prevalent in town, and the other half was for the sympathy Jessica had gained with Liam's temporary suspension.

The party was lifeless and abandoned at intervals by the visitors who'd leave over the excuse of having to cross the haunted Conecuh forest on foot at night. With a multitude of girls lost within the vicinity of the forest, Peter couldn't help but allow them to leave. His lenience wasn't a product of the concern he had for the girls and boys coming to his party, but because he was still thinking about the business. He even had hopes fastened with the organizer's award, so forcing any of the visitors to stay would mean all the blame on him if anything were to happen with the young attendees. So, he let them go whenever they pleased.

Sam, the active member of the Music Society, spent the party night next to Peter in the basement, drinking to his satisfaction with a handful of girls grooving to the spunky beat until he looked down at his wristwatch. The clock read 4:00 a.m.

"It's getting late, buddy," he told Peter.

"What are you saying?" Peter annoyingly inquired.

"I meant," Sam explained, "I'm dizzy and cannot drive home. It would be better if I walk home now before I drop unconscious at the edge of the woods."

"Oh, c'mon, Sam!" Peter grumbled. "We're a team. Forgot what we promised?" he intoned in his boozy state. "The team will stay till the dawn breaks."

"The dawn is expected in an hour, mate. I've done my part and proven my loyalty. Now let me go before I sleep here."

"Don't be a pussy, Sam," Peter sounded scratchy. "You cannot sleep on five vodka shots." He almost spat. "Even if you did, Thomas will drop you home."

Sam looked over at Thomas and chuckled. Peter followed his gaze and sniggered too. "You aren't talking sense, buddy. Look at Thomas," he pointed at the red-headed boy, stumbling his way through the girls and heading for the bar for another shot. "He'll be gone soon."

"Alright," Peter held his hands up. "You can leave, buddy." He struggled to open his droopy eyes but thought better of it. His last words sounded gibberish and contained no vital message, so Sam got going.

Emerging from the club into the velvety darkness of the night, Sam had a fear of the Conecuh forest somewhere deep inside his head. He tried not to speak about it before Peter because he knew any attempt would mean leg-pulling and name-calling for the next day, so he pretty much kept it to himself. Entering the endless loop of darkness around the Conecuh forest, he could sense the unease in the air. His heart was already thudding in his ears, and the booze was beginning to settle in his veins. In a minute or two, he strolled forth with wobbly feet and obscured vision, hoping to reach home safely. Right when he had covered half the distance from Peter's place up North and reached the stretch of the forest, he saw someone he knew.

"Who is it?" he mouthed, almost in a whisper. Squinting through his obscured vision, he tried to decipher the person breaking into the thick forest. Judging from the appearance, he could tell it was a girl, but the route she was taking left him with questions. Now, what kind of girl would return from prom and throw herself into the thick of the woods? he thought. Inching towards her without drawing attention to himself, he struggled to make out the person heading for the forest. What is that? he asked himself. A wheeler bag? It was so dark outside that he could barely tell where she was going. At precisely that moment, Karen whipped around to see if someone was spying on her. As far as her sight could stretch in the pitch darkness, nothing fell in her peripheral vision beyond the stretch of trees.

Sam couldn't believe his eyes. "Karen!" he let out; his voice was hardly above an incoherent mumble. He had half a mind to follow her into the dark forest, but judging from afar, he could tell that wasn't going to be a good idea.

By the time he made his decision to follow her inside, she had disappeared out of sight. Sam wouldn't have panicked if she had been enveloped by the looming darkness of the woods slowly. But her disappearance was quick; one moment she was there, and the next, she wasn't. She breezed past a dilute patch of trees outlining the forest and soon disintegrated into nothing. Just a couple of minutes ago, she was there, dragging her wheeled bag into the woods.

A plethora of questions invaded Sam's mind. Outside the woods, the frequent rustling of bushes and the howling of the wolves pierced through the sky. Sam could also hear the wailing winds. He didn't know how to react to this. His first instinct was to follow, and so he did, but what for? She was gone. He still headed for the forest and saw a ring of smoke diffusing into thin air. Nothing made sense to him. He shook his head in disapproval and decided to take this occurrence as another nightmare from his drunken state.

Little did he know that it wasn't over yet. Returning from the mouth of the Conecuh forest after Karen's sudden disappearance, he marched forth. His eyes were getting droopier, his stride fatigue-bound, and his legs heavier and wobblier with every step he took. As he shuffled along the empty road parallel to the woods, he looked up, and something strange met his eyes.

Some seventy-five yards away to the left of him stood another figure walking in the opposite direction. Sam saw him a split second before he caught sight of him. Just when he did, he jerked his shoulders up, amazed at the sight of Sam as he mirrored him. Sam laughed out loud at the possibility of finding his reflection in a three-dimensional setting. Suppressing his shock, he gave the anonymous figure a little wave that meant the 'oh-you-too-startled-me-haha-sorry' sort of thing. The grotesque figure, on the other hand, just stood there motionless. His eyes were malevolently affixed on Sam, and so were Sam's on the shady

man, thinking that he would wave back or just laugh it away. But nothing came. It felt like forever; the way glances were exchanged between the two in the desolate woods. In the pitch darkness. At 4:18 a.m.

Sam didn't sense the danger until the grotesque stranger opened his mouth to reveal pearl-white rodent teeth between the statement, "Get the fuck out of here. Now!"

He suddenly felt prickles swarming beneath his clothes. Without another thought, he turned around and strolled along the path leading to his home. The weird man watched him from a distance. Drunk, stoned, and paranoid, Sam felt his situation taking a toll on him. He sensed the adrenaline rush in his body and wondered if his scenario was a reality or just another work of imagination. Just when he was about to break into a run, he looked over his shoulder and saw the stranger's eyes turning blood red. A scream escaped his mouth before springing forth with all his

strength while the mysterious figure adopted the speed of light.

The very next minute, the sinister figure was standing ahead of Sam. More like a car, ungeared for the brake, he bumped into what felt like the ice body of the shady man and fell on all fours.

VampTown

"WELCOME!" the vampires intoned.

As the lights flicked on, all eyes fell in perfect sync on the only beautiful creature present in the clubhouse. Karen. Of course, they were all oblivious to her blood type! Cancer also organized things in a manner that wouldn't surface any clue related to her identity. For the time being, he too was mesmerized by the beauty of young Karen. She had the movie star look, not overly tall and willowy to exude masculine vibes. If anything, her muscle definition was perfect and her stride stacked with elegance. The first thing

everyone noticed on her face was the unusual peachy skin, more like silk over the glass, which craved the hunger pangs of many men. Only that they mistook it for hotness. She was the kind of girl that aroused the feeling of envy in every other woman. Slowly as she strode forth, away from the patch of vampires standing close, she exuberated youth and looked like an epitome of beauty in the black flowing gown.

Cancer sensed her uneasiness and asked the Vamitooth to continue the welcome ceremony. Listening to this, Damien, the organizer of the concert, skidded to a halt before Karen, bending down on his knees.

"Miss Karen," he said, stretching his hand out, asking for the honor of having her on stage. "Would you mind getting on stage and jamming up with our musicians?"

Karen felt her first wave of nerves but gave her hand as a gesture of approval. As soon as Damien held her hand, he sensed the hot and fleshy skin against his ice-cold

skin and felt the hair on the back of his neck stand up. He worked up the nerve to mount Karen on the stage while the vampires clapped hysterically over the excitement of hearing her sing. After letting go of her hand, Damien immediately walked around the boundary that was keeping the vampires back and reached Cancer.

"Sir!" Damien said hastily.

"Yes, Dami," Cancer stated. Reading the concern on his face for a bit, he allowed, "All okay?"

"I'm not sure, sir."

"What do you mean?" Cancer inquired, too anxious to hear about the secret he had kept.

"This girl, sir," Damien panted and looked over at Karen on stage, nervously smiling. "There is something wrong about her. I can sense it."

"Oh, it's nothing," Cancer assured him, trying hard not to let his expressions give away the secret.

"It is, sir." Damien paused upon sensing the panicky rise in his voice and toned down. "This girl is different.

She isn't among us; I can assure you. And I'm telling you this because I have my loyalty to you. I don't want trouble for you. She is," he paused again and glanced around to see if anyone was listening; everyone was busy watching Karen as one by one the band members arrived. "She is a human, I feel. Her blood type smelled sweet as I took her hand and kissed it. Moreover, her skin emits warm radiations."

"How can you say that?" Cancer strictly asked, half disappointed that Damien had easily identified her.

"That's because I am a doctor too. I can easily tell the diseases or any other vampire condition from smelling the blood type. She isn't one of us, and I can assure you that by smelling her blood composition."

Cancer glanced around to see if anyone had heard what Damien said, then quickly took him by the arm and dragged him to a corner. "Damien!" he said. "You promise me that you won't tell anybody about her identity."

"Sir!" Damien said astoundingly. "Did you know already?"

"Yes, I do," Cancer curtly said. "She's here for a purpose. A bigger purpose!" he pressed. "She'll go back to her region soon. Besides, she is a Goth descendant. We can't harm her. Remember what Lord Byron said?"

"Yes, I do, but—"

"That's it," Cancer intervened. "Nothing more on this. And I trust you like my brother, Damien. I know you won't tell anyone, let alone intend any harm to her."

"I won't," Damien assured and went backstage again.

Meanwhile, Karen was on stage and glancing over at the vampires she had known from the social site. She spotted Zobray from the stage and waved at him. Zobray beamed at her and waved back. Karen began to gain her confidence as the vampires cheered and couldn't wait for her to sing.

Cancer had his eyes fixated on Karen, and a look of panic was evident on his face. He didn't want his true identity as Karen to unravel before any of the vampires. He had brainstormed about the safest hotel in VampTown to ensure her safety. He had also arranged for healthy human cuisine so she would not die of starvation there. One thing that he didn't tell Karen, Lazarus, or anyone in VampTown was how he went down into the forest of Conecuh while Karen was about to set off for their town.

Though he told Karen to reach the Conecuh forest at 4:00 a.m., he wasn't comfortable with the idea of calling a girl to the woods at such a time. For one thing, he didn't trust the vampires who were forever on a hunt, looking for girl blood in Conecuh; he didn't want any of them to hunt Karen down before she made it up there. Another factor he knew was how unsafe it was for girls to roam around at night in Alabama City from the street crime point of view. So, he couldn't risk calling Karen to his world at such an inappropriate time and place.

Known for his protective nature, Cancer didn't hesitate to travel down and ensure her safe departure. A minute later, he spotted Sam and misinterpreted his intentions for her. Unlike others, he didn't kill the boy; instead, he only tried his best to scare and shoo him away. Another radar that blared in his mind was related to the boy who witnessed Karen's departure. If he did see the smoke ring, the vampire world could get in trouble. Karen would also be questioned upon her return to Alabama City as to how she went where she went.

Cancer decided to store the worries for himself and ponder over them later. He didn't want to inform her about what had happened when she was leaving her town. Soon, Karen was handed the mic by one of the band members, and she began singing in her melodious voice. Her soothing voice recovered Cancer from his anxiety and brought him back to the present. His beam grew wider on watching his plan falling back into place.

Karen was a performer! She was covering every space

on stage to interact with her audience. The vampires, on the other hand, were transported to another world by her melodious voice. They couldn't stop swaying back and forth over the symphony of her musical voice. Millions of colors were shooting out like a spectrum from a mysterious disco ball; its glow looked like that of a star on a clear night. The moon was perched atop the sky, admiring and projecting its dusty rays down at the big noisy concert.

In a matter of minutes, Karen hit something. In her stupor, she didn't know that the mic holder had a sharp spike at its edge. After rocking back and forth the stage for a bit, when she placed the mic back in its holder, the edgy spike pierced her wrist. The very next moment, one by one, all the vampires opened their eyes. Oblivious to what had happened, Karen kept on singing. But this time around, the once awestruck look on the faces of the audience had transformed into shocking contempt. Slowly, the blood on her wrist dripped down her ankle, and soon she sensed something wrong.

The entire clubhouse was filled with the delicious aroma of warm honey blood, and the vampires wiped their lips off their tongues. She stopped singing all of a sudden, ripped the cloth off her gown, and wrapped it around her wrist to stop the bleeding. Too late. The vampires already had their mouths gaped open in shock, horror, hunger, contempt, and disappointment. Cancer couldn't believe his eyes. His plan of keeping her identity a secret was all in shambles. He knew that in no time, the vampires would try and attack her. And that he had to do something quickly, but what? He cudgeled his brains, but nothing came.

Zobray was also stunned by the unexpected disclosure of her friend's secret. He recalled all the times he had spoken to her on the internet. Never once did he fathom that his friend was a human.

"A human?" he mouthed.

He wheeled around and glanced over at Cancer, who was now holding his head out of nervousness. Zobray quickly sprinted in his direction and spoke about the matter. Unlike others, he didn't rant about how shocked he was at discovering her identity. Instead, his first question instilled a flair of relief in the otherwise chaotic mind of Cancer.

"Sir?" Zobray panted. "How do we save Karen now?"

Cancer blankly stared at him. No great idea was crossing his mind. Reading the tension in his demeanor, Zobray took the situation in his stride and dashed for the stage. Reaching the stage was a big struggle in itself. Almost the entire VampTown was there for the concert, and to Karen's shame, everyone saw the way her lie was detected. The audience marveled over her courage with quite disdain, as despite being a human, she climbed the stage confidently and sang her vocals out. Above all, the confidence with which she made it to the vampire world was amazing, irrespective of the fact that vampires share a thirst for honey-aroma blood.

Library broke through the hordes of the crowd in an attempt to save Karen. At the same time, some vampires had already reached the stage and were surrounding Karen from all corners. For no apparent reason, the musicians tried to convince the vampires to let her be. They beseeched everyone to forgive her, but the horde kept circling her from all sides. All of them revealed their rodent teeth and lolled their tongues to one side – a gesture of exhibiting hunger.

Karen's state was indecipherable. Her watery eyes widened, and the hair on the back of her neck rose. She felt a gaggle of gooseflesh erupting out of her frigid, naked skin. She struggled to scream, but all she managed was an incoherent mumble; the inside of her mouth sucked all the moisture. The vampires loomed near from all sides, watching the peachy skin, sensing the emission of her warm breath, and moaning over the delicious aroma of her warm honey blood. Quite evidently, she saw the irresistible urge to devour her blood in the demeanor of the vampires. Her head swam, her scalp prickled, and in no time, she passed out.

~

12:00 p.m. Alabama City, Police Station

Sam worked up the courage to visit the police station and report what he saw. He would also confess his misdeed of getting drunk overnight, yet walking down the empty road of Conecuh Forest. Traveling down this route was otherwise deemed an offense under law no. 55. He reached the station and informed the front desk officer that he was there to report something serious.

"Yes, young boy," the freckle-skinned front desk man said. "What are you here for?"

Sam glanced over at the name of the officer that read, 'Mr. Clarke Wittington,' and continued.

"Mr. Clarke! I am here to confess something. I broke the law, but more than that," he swallowed hard. "I came here with what I witnessed yesterday in the Conecuh Forest."

Clarke carefully eyed Sam up and down and then pulled out the pen and paper to write it all down. "Start with the law. Which crime have you committed?"

"I attended a Halloween party yesterday and drank vodka to my satisfaction. Since the venue was set in the North Conecuh, I knew I had to cross past the haunted forest alone and on foot."

"I don't suspect that a crime if there was no alternate route you could take home," Clarke explained. "Still, kid. You must avoid that road. Many incidents have occurred there, and the government can't risk having another disappearance case."

"But it is there," Sam confidently said. "I saw Karen disappearing into the woods."

Clarke carefully studied the boy's confidence and almost chuckled. "Kid," he let out jovially. "You were drunk! How can you be so sure?"

"If you don't believe me, search out Karen Lewis and see for yourself where she is."

Sophia was too pissed at what Karen did. She couldn't quite budge from the anger of how forcefully Karen submitted their project. And now Sophia was two hundred percent sure that her friend was hiding something. Despite the submission, she decided to find out what it was. She knew Karen wouldn't be home, and

Laura had been to her place over a hundred times, so she wouldn't mind if Sophia asked to share her PC for a bit. With that, she set off for Karen's place with all the hopes to figure out what her friend had been keeping a secret.

After fifteen minutes, she was at her doorstep, ringing her doorbell. Laura opened the door a while later.

"Oh, hello, dear!" Laura said softly.

"Hello," Sophia said sweetly. "Mind if I come in?"

"Sure," Laura said as she allowed her in. "But do you know Karen is off for a vacation?"

"Oh, so I do. It's just that I wanted to use her PC." Laura gestured for her to sit in the living room. "Thank you. We were working on a project together. She entrusted me with it as she left, but now my PC isn't working."

"Not a problem, dear," Laura said politely. "It's your home." Just then, the doorbell rang. "Now, who is it?" Laura paced to the door, and Sophia also stood up and headed for Karen's room.

"Inspector Clark from Alabama Station!" He pulled out his ID card. Sophia stopped midway to listen to what the police were doing at her home.

"Yes?" Laura asked anxiously. "What is it?"

"We're here over the report of Karen's disappearance submitted by an eyewitness," Inspector Clark said.

"You must be mistaken, Inspector," Laura chuckled. "Karen isn't missing. She's off on a vacation to Huntsville."

"We aren't mistaken, ma'am," Clark plainly said. "We've done all the investigation. There were no flight departure records for this place. If anything," the inspector paused and then stated with a sigh, "this place doesn't exist in the first place."

Laura had her eyes bawling out of their sockets while Sophia almost forgot how to shut her mouth. She recalled all that her friend had said, the excuses she'd been making, and the site they accidentally opened up. She felt the earth sweeping beneath her feet, and apprehension gripped her over the concern for her friend.

CHAPTER 8
THE SAVIOR

The vampires were slowly looming near from all corners, trying to study Karen and her species. Her sweet blood was attracting and inviting more of them to drink. Some younger ones had already reached the stairs leading to the stage; they couldn't beat the thirst and hunger with Karen's blood smelling like pure, raw honey extract. Some of them, who felt the stair route would take too long, climbed up the stage from the front and the diagonal corner, giving in to their temptation. The others took the time and energy to walk around the long hallway leading to the backstage, which was also an easy doorway to the front of the stage if it weren't for the distance covered.

Karen, on the other hand, couldn't feel her limbs out of fear. A familiar numbness settled in her bones, and she thought she would lose balance anytime now. It all seemed like a nightmare. One moment she was in her town, living peacefully with Laura with no evident threats to her life, and due to one wrong decision, she was at the mouth of brutal death. She chose this for herself despite Sophie's warning. It was always her curiosity that made her do stupid things, make unhealthy choices, and take lethal decisions. She once had an encounter with a psychotic ghost and had almost been ripped open from the flesh if it hadn't been for a priest saving her at the last moment.

Here, there was no one to save her. She had traveled from Alabama City to VampTown just to taste a death that suited her dauntless nature. But on top of it all, one couldn't deny her foolishness for walking into the mousetrap herself. Too silly of her to believe all the stories Laura had narrated to her despite her frame of mind, too naïve to trust Cancer while following her instincts, and too confident to think that she was untouchable. Now that she was there, serving herself on the platter for the blood-thirsty monsters, all of it came in flashes. One question that kept throbbing at the back of her mind was related to Cancer. Despite the numbness and overwhelming palpitations, she worked up the nerve to look out for him in the crowd.

A few seconds of face-scanning and there he was, staring back at her blankly. His face was utterly void of expressions. It was as if Karen's gaze affixed on him, recalling all that he had said on the video call.

"We have found that you're a Gothic descendant yourself. We intend no harm," his voice replayed fresh in her head. *"We owe Gothics our lives for how they sacrificed themselves during the Battle of Trinix and proved their loyalty."* Suddenly Karen doubted the intent of the words delivered to her.

"Your parents, James and Bella Lewis, also fought like warriors without caring about their infant daughter." The memory of him pausing and wiping a tear surfaced in her head. The tear? Was it all a pretense? *"For this reason, we want to pay back. Therefore, we've decided to invite you over to our world to stay forever. Would you like to come? We'll give you a grand tour of our place and greet you like our very own people."* Suddenly all the words lost meaning.

Cancer had his mind buzzing. He couldn't think straight. Nothing was coming to his memory. He didn't possess the powers of his grandfather, Lord Byron, who had once dealt with such a situation by lulling the vampires to sleep. He knew no such spell or mantra. But there was one spell that his grandfather had taught him to escape any panicky situation, and that was to *seize the moment.*

"Seize the moment," Cancer mouthed aloud with a sudden realization. That was it! He now knew what to do. He glanced over at Karen again, who looked hopeless and petrified. The swarm of vampires was now standing next to her, eyeing her up and down like a predator does before attacking. Zobray was now at the stairs leading to the stage.

Cancer immediately closed his eyes, yelled the spell, "Seizopodium Lataraadish!" and pointed his palm towards the ones surrounding Karen. The next second, everyone on the stage was deadly still except for Karen and Zobray. Cancer also cast the same spell on the remaining audience in the hall until everything and everyone was paused except for the three of them. Zobray was amazed, fathoming what had just happened, and Karen was batting her lashes endlessly, her mouth open. Zobray quickly turned and looked over at Cancer in the distance. He immediately knew it was him.

"Thank you, master," he said aloud, bowing slightly in respect. Cancer nodded and began striding in the direction of the stage. Advancing forth, he started instructing Zobray on what his next step should be.

"Take her home. Your home. The hotel I've booked is no longer safe, I presume. She'll be safe at your place. Do keep me updated about her safety until I arrange for some other place for her residence."

"Sure, master," Zobray said, bowing again.

Cancer turned to face Karen. His eyes exhibited guilt

and shame. "I don't have words to express my regret and remorse for getting you in this trouble. I had it all planned out. I didn't anticipate this. I'm extremely sorry for the inconvenience, Karen."

Karen looked down at her feet and didn't reply.

Zobray bowed again and left with Karen.

~

Alabama City - 9:00 p.m.

The streets were abandoned. Not a shadow of a human to be seen. No car was observed rolling past the roads. Nature was left alone to breathe without the polluted fumes of the vehicles or chemical industry. Trees still swayed to the music of the breeze, waves still produced high tides, the sun still rose from the east and went down the west, and all other species continued with their regular patterns of living except for humans. They were bound to live within the confines of their homes because of a deadly disease outbreak: COVID-19, an infectious disease caused by a coronavirus and transmitted through droplets of an infected person's coughs, sneezes, and exhales.

The infected person was observed to have a fever, dry cough, fatigue, sore throat, headache, chest pain/pressure, shortness of breath, and loss of speech/movement. For this reason, the government of Alabama City announced the complete lockdown of the city. They further announced specific preventive measures that included wearing masks and gloves, washing one's hands or bathing after human interaction, avoiding gatherings and meetups amid the pandemic, and meeting people from a distance. Almost everyone followed the government's guidelines except for some who had to run essential errands. One such person to go out to buy his baby's diaper was Alex.

At around 9:00 p.m., he was done with buying items for his household and was returning home. He took all preventive measures seriously, which was why he had his mask and gloves on. He even avoided taking the road down the Conecuh Forest, yet the alternate route had other horrors in store for him. Walking down the lane, he sensed a shadow whooshing past his back. Feeling the cold air on his neck, he whipped around quickly, but there was nothing. He strode forth, faster this time as he knew what this could mean. He paced along the street, praying for his breath to avoid the creature if it were the same one the others had lost their lives to. He still felt that someone was following him. He dared not look over his shoulder and waste time and instead focused on reaching home as soon as possible. Just when he was hardly three minutes away from his home, a dark figure came in front of him.

Alex wiped the sweat off his forehead, and the grotesque creature impersonated his movement. He broke a cold sweat and paced towards his home, but the beast blocked his way again. He smiled and muttered, "Where are you going, honey? Don't you know I'm hungry?"

Alex attempted to push the six-foot-tall creature who had a human-like appeal except for the rodent teeth, blood-red eyes, and white skin. The beast was invincible and too strong to beat down. Just then, he took the time to grab Alex by the neck and bit down on it to suck the blood. Alex yelled his vocals out, but no one could hear, let alone help him on the vacant street, as everyone was concerned about their own lives. The threats were fatal. First, it was vampires, and the latest one was COVID-19. None were willing to sacrifice their lives. The vampire who hunted him down was also oblivious to the disease outbreak and mindlessly sucked on the blood of a COVID-19 patient. Little did he know what trouble he had invited for his VampTown.

CHAPTER 9

CORONA OUTBREAK

Sophia hadn't been at peace since the day she heard about Karen's disappearance. Her thoughts and concerns were focused on her friend, fathoming the state she would be in if she were in a vampire's cage. They had not gotten along in the last couple of days before her disappearance, and Sophia knew it was her fault, which is why she had apologized. She didn't understand why Karen couldn't forgive her, though. Suddenly, the pangs of regret made her shoot up abruptly and get to her feet. Back and forth she strode, faster each second as the ugly thoughts of her friend's state gripped her.

She emerged from her room and onto the open terrace to escape the suffocation. She contemplated her friend's whereabouts, and the horrible flashes of that spooky site crossed her mind. "I'm sure this website has something to do with her disappearance or —" She didn't want to think about the worst. "Is she alive?" A question popped up in her head and gifted her gooseflesh in turn. Though the night was a reward of sorts as the refreshing breezes carried the fragrance of flowers and only tranquility could be observed far and wide, yet the tornado was flaring up in Sophia's mind.

The cool winds of the terrace failed to lend her the little solace she expected and gave her shivers instead. At that moment, something crossed her mind, and she hurried into her room. She looked up at the clock that read 9:10 p.m., pulled out the evening coat from the dresser, took the keys to her bike, and set off.

9:15 p.m.

Laura was seated in her usual spot in the rocking chair opposite the television. The channel was tuned into a musical gala showing a lady wailing at the top of her lungs and attempting what the elders call 'opera.' Laura had her eyes on the TV, but her mind was somewhere else. She couldn't shake the information Inspector Carl gave her upon visiting her home.

"Ms. Laura," he said and paused. "Please allow me inside to have this conversation with you."

Laura, who was already too shocked about Karen lying to her about a place that didn't exist, allowed him in without forethought – probably in anticipation of knowing more about her granddaughter. "Please, come in," she said.

Inspector Clark got in, and so did Sam. Laura, who didn't know the schoolmate of Karen, allowed him in too, confusing him for just another inspector. Both Sam and Clark were in their casual dresses, so one couldn't distinguish their identity until they revealed their ID cards. The conversation halted until the three of them settled down in the living room.

Sophie didn't sit on the couch; she preferred standing in the distance until Laura called her out.

"Dear," she said in a quavering voice. "Did you hear what Inspector Clark said?" Sophie nodded. Laura's face suddenly exhibited hope as she asked, "Did Karen tell you where she was heading to?"

Sophie looked down at the floor. As much as she wished for the ground to crack open, burying her along with the guilt of her relations with her friend, she also wanted to know what had happened to Karen. So, she kept quiet.

"Is she a friend?" Inspector Clark asked Laura as he looked over at her.

Before Laura could respond, Sam intervened, "Well, yes! She's her best friend."

"Oh, would you please have a seat with us?" Clark requested. Laura also gestured to her in urgency to have a seat. Sophie quietly did as she was told.

"So," Inspector Clark continued, "what did she tell you about the vacation?"

"Nothing," Laura informed. "She just said that she was going on a tour to Huntsville for ten days and," she paused and tried to recall, "and yeah, that she had applied for the trip through a site in which she'd be surrounded by people she did not know, but she trusted the organization who had arranged this trip."

"Okay," Clark said. "Is there anything else that she discussed with you before leaving, Ms. Laura? Or did you observe anything weird and panicky in her tone or demeanor?"

"Uh," Laura cudgeled her brain, and her memory started receding to the entire scenario of that day. "Yeah, she told me that she was missing her parents and—what did Vamp—" She paused. A sudden realization left her aghast. She replayed the entire conversation she had with her and suddenly comprehended where her granddaughter would be.

Sophia shifted uneasily in her position despite hearing only half the word 'Vamp.' She knew what it could mean.

"Vamp, what?" Inspector Clark inquired. He observed as Laura began to zone out. "Please continue with what you were saying, Ms. Laura," he intervened before she could delve deep into her thoughts or decide not to provide them with the information they needed.

Too late. Laura had changed her mind. She perceived Inspector Clark as a threat of sorts who could put them in prison or send them both to a museum and charge tickets upon seeing Laura and Karen, who had their history and loyalty associated with the Vampires.

"Just that she was missing her parents and needed some time out from her routine," she covered.

"Okay," Clark said as he conjured up the right words to communicate to this lady. "So, the thing is there is no such place as Huntsville, to begin with, and this boy, Sam—" he placed a hand on Sam's shoulder—"he saw Karen disappearing into oblivion right before his eyes."

"Yeah, one moment she was there at the edge of the forest in a black gown, and the very next second, she disintegrated and disappeared," Sam informed.

"Well, that's insane!" Laura remarked. "Were you

drunk then, boy? Because what you saw defies every law of convention."

"I just had one or two shots," Sam defended. "But believe me, this is true. I was sober enough to make out what was happening."

"Bullshit," Laura retorted. She turned to face Clark and said, "It was nice meeting you, Inspector. I understand your concerns, and I appreciate that too, but I have complete faith that my Karen will return." She stood up in an attempt to show the door to both guests. "Next time you drop in, that is ten days later, which I'm sure you wouldn't because my granddaughter will be back by then. But if she wouldn't, hope you'll come forth with valid proofs and evidence."

Both Inspector Clark and Sam exchanged glances and stood up. "Well, hope we don't have to, but if we do, I hope I'll be able to satisfy you with my findings," Inspector Clark said. "Thanks for your time."

The two of them headed for the door, and Laura closed it behind them. Sophia was still seated on the couch when Laura was shoving them out the door. She came back and took her place next to Sophia.

"Dear," she purred while taking Sophia's hand in hers. "Did you see what they're up to?"

Laura still thought Sophia was a Goth descendant—at least that was what Karen had told her. Sophia couldn't believe that Karen hadn't revealed her in front of Laura. Laura was comfortable discussing the truth in front of her.

"Not exactly," Sophia mouthed. "What do you feel?"

"Dear," Laura got started. "I did have a conversation with Karen. She didn't tell me the truth about where she was heading, but she gave me hints."

"What do you mean?" Sophia inquired.

"The day she was planning to set out on this tour, she came to me and dug me for details about VampTown," Laura briefed her.

"What were her questions exactly, and what did you say?" Sophia asked.

Laura told her everything. That was when everything began to make sense for Sophia. Now she knew why her friend was so upset with her. She quietly listened to what Laura had to say and decided to protect her friend's secret for life and track her whereabouts sooner or later. She had left quietly that day with a promise to herself to come back again and go over her PC to dig out that site. She did keep her promise despite the pandemic and lockdown.

The clock struck 9:30 p.m., and the doorbell to Laura's

residence rang. She muted the live opera on television and reached for the door.

"Oh, hello, dear," Laura greeted. "Is everything okay?"

"Yes, granny," Sophia stated. "May I come in?"

"Oh," Laura gave her head a quick tap. "Silly me. Of course, dear. Come on in."

Sophia entered. Laura showed her the living room.

"I'm amazed you made it here at this hour, especially amid the lockdown. Wait! You aren't wearing your mask either."

Sophia smirked. "I've heard it hasn't spread here much. The other countries have it worse."

"Still, dear," Laura sounded concerned. "You should be careful. You're too young to contract this shit."

"Don't worry," Sophia smiled. "I'm not infected."

"Oh, love!" Laura beamed back. "Do you think I'm afraid of death? If anything, I'm more than willing to embrace it soon to meet my son, James," she sighed. "I'm only speaking about your health and safety."

"Don't be so willing," Sophia said softly. "Karen loves you a lot. I'm sure she wouldn't be able to survive alone. She needs you."

"Why do you think I'm alive, Sophia?" Laura pointed.

"She is my only reason for living. I hope she makes it back here soon. If she is where I think she is, she'll be taken care of."

Sophia smiled. "I know what she means to you. She is my family too, and that's one reason why I'm here. I think I know where she is."

"Really?" Laura asked excitedly. "Please tell me it's VampTown."

"So it is, I feel. But I hope she is safe," Sophia sighed. "Would you mind if I use her PC because this is where I think all of it started."

"Sure, dear," Laura stood up and got into her room. She came outside with a small colorful key bunch. "Here you go. The black one."

"Thank you, Granny." Sophia took the keys, got into her friend's room, and opened her PC first thing.

~

VampTown

10:30 p.m.

Karen was living at Zobrey's place. Cancer still couldn't arrange for a hotel or a place for Karen's stay, given the amount of safety she needed. Aubrey's place was comfortable too. He lived alone in a house containing four rooms. The details of the house weren't anything like the house in Alabama City. The vampires lived differently.

Zobrey's room consisted of a dark wooden dresser that matched the color of his stylish coffin stacked with a soft mattress. The guest room in which Karen was staying didn't contain a coffin but rather a mattress and a pillow. There was a dresser too, with an attached mirror and a small gym area that Zobrey hadn't checked out ever since Karen dropped in. The walls of her room contained the quotations and verses of Lord Byron and some pictures of the scary places Zobrey had visited.

Karen was sick. Since the day Zobrey had brought her over, she hadn't been well. Her fever, together with chest tightness and shortness of breath, kept increasing and made her bedridden. Day by day, her condition only worsened. She started losing weight and would sleep all day long and wake up at night. Zobrey even provided her with a phone that she didn't get a chance to explore much, given the fatigue that gripped her. She avoided using a cell phone since the mere glance at the screen was giving her a severe headache.

10:30 p.m., and she sensed a knock on the door. She slowly rose to a sitting position and then responded, "Yes."

"Hello, young lady," Zobrey popped his head in from the door and then moved in with a food trolley for Karen. "How are you feeling now?" he beamed.

"Much better," Karen smiled. "What do we have for dinner today?"

"Corn soup and mashed potato," Zobrey said enthusiastically. "I don't guarantee you the taste again since I'm not used to cooking. Trust me, I couldn't tell potato and corn apart either until my mini research," he sniggered.

"I owe you a lot for all of this, Zobrey," Karen said. "You're truly a friend."

"Well, thanks, madame!" he said in his typical energetic tone. He passed the food tray to Karen.

"By the way," Karen said as she received it, "Tell me something. Why aren't you tempted to have my blood just like the other vampires?"

"Well, there are reasons for that," he explained. "Number one: my mother was a Goth, and my father was a vampire. My mother would have her typical humane meals while my father would get down on the ground to suck the blood of humans. I think the cross of two unique creatures resulted in me," he winked. "I mean, I turned out to be an organic vampire who likes having to munch down two or three human meals and, at the same time, loves drinking deer's blood." He shrugged. "So, for both reasons, I'm not tempted the way other vampires are," he winked.

"Finally, someone I can trust," Karen sighed.

"Well, you can't," he jovially said. "Given the fact that I am a guy, I can be tempted in other ways too, so what if not for the blood."

"Whoa! I'm scared," Karen jokingly let out. "By the way, bringing me food day in and day out and having me in your house does not give you the official permission to flirt," she sportingly said.

"Well, I don't see anything wrong in mingling with a pretty human," he teased. "Please allow me to maintain the vamp-human reunion legacy, Karen. Only you can help me do that," he winked.

"I would have helped you if I hadn't been a black belt or a feminist for that matter," Karen joked.

"Now I'm scared," he laughed. "By the way, lady. You're so hot that even I'm beginning to feel a little fever and headache now."

"Well, let me admit," Karen laughed, "that was the only punchline I agreed with."

"You'll begin to agree with more of them. Just wait and watch!" Zobrey flamboyantly remarked.

"HAHA… in your dreams," Karen replied. Just then, Zobrey's phone began to ring.

"Well, dreams do come true," Zobrey winked as he pulled out his phone from his pocket and slid to answer. "Yes, master!"

Karen instantly knew it was Cancer on the other end of the phone. Her eyes and ears were affixed on Zobrey, trying to make out the conversation between them. After listening on the phone for two minutes, Zobrey suddenly turned around and looked over at Karen with a concerned look.

1:30 a.m.

A week before.

Vampire Rex made it back to VampTown and into his home. After quite a long time, he'd had the best dinner. Alex's blood tasted like heaven. He wondered why the people of Alabama City had stopped going out at all. Finding prey was quite a struggle this time because of the void streets and roads. He thanked the heavens for sending a man out of nowhere. Unlike other vampires, Rex didn't take much time in scaring his prey, which almost every other vampire would enjoy and take pride in discussing in the mic drop. As for him, he was too hungry and thirsty to play before consuming his feast. He quickly gave in to his temptations and immediately got to business.

On returning home, he looked for his grandfather – the only family he had.

"Oh, here you are!" Rex paced toward his grandfather, who was busy playing a video game.

"Hello, macho! Where have you been?" the grandpa asked.

"Downtown. Hunting down a prey," he winked, but grandpa had his attention on the video game. Rex came to him and kissed him on his forehead.

"Whoa! Rex is a big boy now," he exclaimed. He put his video game aside. "Come on, make your grandpa proud and tell me how you scared your prey?"

"Ah. Grandpa, I gave in to my temptations this time," Rex sighed.

"Such a disappointment, buddy!" Grandpa grunted.

"Sorry. It's just that I couldn't find my prey down there. I waited for three hours in camouflage, but nobody came except this unlucky guy."

"I trust you, boy," Grandpa shrugged. "Better luck next time." He picked up his cell phone again and got busy playing his favorite video game.

"I will not disappoint you next time, grappa!" Rex jovially said and hurried into his room. He quickly got fresh, changed his clothes, and left for the party with his friends.

He danced and enjoyed the night away with his friends, oblivious to the virus he'd contracted. One after another, he infected whichever individual he crossed or danced with. Almost a week later, his grandfather fell sick. His situation started getting worse with every passing day. Even Rex took him to the doctor, but none could diagnose his disease. The doctors who checked him and came in any kind of contact with him also started showing the same symptoms. As for Rex, he was too sick, but he dragged himself somehow from one hospital to another to save his grandfather, but he couldn't. He died the very next week.

Rex, who was also sick, remained inside his room as weakness gripped him. He couldn't get up, let alone hunt down any person in Alabama City. He tried doing his magic spell to bring deer meat or blood but to no avail. His magical powers were diffusing into nothing. Then came the day when he transformed into a bat that secreted a sticky, gooey serum in his bed. Now all he had to do was starve and silently wait for his death if it were to come. Rex unknowingly sucked the blood of an infected human and carried the germ to

VampTown. Anyone he came in contact with was affected and sick. The disease spread like wildfire in VampTown, and no one knew what was happening. The younger ones were losing their power, and the older ones were dying, succumbing to this virus.

CHAPTER 10
VAMPTOWN DISCOVERY

10:00 p.m., June 2, 2020, Monday

Clara was late. She was the manager of operations at a reputed organization and had her work timings from 1:00 p.m. to 7:00 p.m. Despite the lockdown, the managers were supposed to visit the office to assign tasks to their employees sitting at home. Clara went for the same reason. Unfortunately, that day, a meeting was summoned last minute by the department head, and Clara had to stay back and attend it along with other officials. She didn't realize how fast the time paced, and before she knew it, the clock struck 10:00 p.m.

The meeting took forever to finish. It finally did at 10:13 p.m., and everyone headed home. Clara, too, was out in the parking lot when she found her car tire punctured. "Darn!" she spat and looked around. "Everyone has gone." She meandered out of the parking area and emerged into the thick dark velvet of the night. "What shall I do? Mom will be very mad at me."

"Taxi!" she called out to an empty yellow car standing in the distance. "Tax…" she trailed off. "Nah, too expensive. I should take the train instead." And so, she did. She headed for the train station that was only a five-minute walk from her office. The road looked long abandoned, with not a soul to be seen. The nightfall cocooned her in its protective fold. As she strolled along, cool breezes swept the alienated street, leaving her with disquieting chills. Amid shudders, she rubbed her arms and hands to get whatever warmth it could lend. Up above the ground, thick, murky clouds covered half the sky. And right beneath them, owls and bats silently swept overhead. The road was quiet and dark; even shadows were swallowed by the encroaching darkness.

Soon, she entered the less crowded train station. At that moment, there was no train present on the platform. She strode for the counter perched in the corner to know about the next set-off details. The exceptionally lean man sitting at the counter informed her that the next train was going to be around in twenty minutes. Clara sighed and took her place on a seat across from the platform. She waited for hardly two minutes before dozing off.

Paper rustled. She woke up. She yawned and rubbed the sleep out of her eyes. On making out the scene around her, she realized that the fraction of people left at the station was gone. "Dammit," she shot up. "How long have I been asleep? Have I missed my train?" She glanced down at her wristwatch. "Unbelievable! I think I've missed it." She glanced around and heard the scuttling of the engine against the metal platform. But nothing in sight. "Yes! Yes. I think the train is coming," she heaved a sigh of relief. A few seconds later, a train glided along the subway station and emerged into sight. Clara was elated that finally, she'd reach home now. The day had been too exhausting for her; she hardly got the time to scratch her head either. Her employees had kept her busy with calls and queries, and her department head bombarded her with project analysis at intervals. That was too much work for a young starter like her to manage. This was her first shot at managing.

The train halted at the station. She slid in as the door flung open. The inside of the train was a void, something that was expected in the middle of the night and amidst the COVID-19 breakout. Only in the distance, a woman was seated in a seat with her grocery bag resting on the floor. Clara looked for an ideal spot to sit on the empty train. She sat far away from the woman. This lady in a light blue kimono was entirely immobile. From a distance, Clara could see red stains at the hem of her dress. Initially, she was confused about the dress design until later. Her hair was long and tied up with a thick pink ribbon.

The train started moving. The engines screeched along the metallic platform, producing a familiar whistle. Soon, an overwhelming sense of slumber settled over her to wash her exhaustion away. She dozed off. A minute later, she dreamed of this woman in a blue kimono coming to her and handing her a photo of a woman. This kimono lady had blood stains on her clothes and a crooked smile. A drip of dried blood was studded on the corner of her lips. She passed a sickening smile in her direction. Clara saw the photo and couldn't look away.

The picture was of her, squashed under the train, and what remained were the sticky, gooey remnants. The photo showed blood all over the place, and her brain matter was crushed into appalling pink stuff. Her eye socket was hollow, and her eyeballs were badly mashed. Her yellowish intestine was coming out of her mouth and meeting the platform. Suddenly and quite abruptly, she woke up. She puffed out heavy breaths. There were beads of sweat on her forehead as she glanced around, desperately searching for the lady. She was gone. Thankfully. She sighed. Relief washed over her. She opened her purse and rummaged through the headphones to connect them to her phone. She sensed movement beside her. He slowly craned her neck to look to her left, and there she was, the kimono lady! But not entirely. Her body wasn't there, but her head was stuck in through the train window. Her revulsive smile was transformed into a grin.

Clara shrieked her vocals out and woke her for real this time. She shot up and ran along the narrow alley of the train. She didn't know what was happening. The train had been moving all this time.

How come this woman managed to step out? And even if she did, how come she gave her head inside the window while her body was out? What's with the dream?

Too many questions occupied her mind. She didn't know where to go. Much that her sight could stretch, she couldn't find a soul on the train. She strode along the narrow pathway parallel to the seats, flinging open the door of one compartment after another, not a passenger to be seen. Quite horrendously, she gazed at the windows and saw speedy trails of the kimono woman, almost like electricity. Clara didn't stop; she kept sprinting in the moving train until the train halted to a stop.

As it did, her insides froze. In that momentary pause, she heard the screech of the train door opening. With that, the surge of adrenaline flushed down her core. The creature that appeared was the kimono woman again. She smiled, and Clara screamed. "You're okay?" said the lean man from the counter.

Clara glanced around in horror. She was still at the station, sitting on a hardwood seat across from the platform—still, no other person at the station except her and the lean counterman.

"Ye… Yeah!" she mouthed. "I think I was dreaming." Her head swam as she tried to fix her gaze.

"Yeah, it's okay," he said and was distracted by the sound of the approaching train. "The train is coming," he stated, looking over at the first trail of moving vehicles on the platform. "Get ready."

The next minute, the train was at the station, and Clara was quietly staring at it with horror. She contemplated taking the taxi instead because now she wouldn't be able to take the train with all the horror awash on her. She stood up, and instead of strolling out the exit, she walked over the yellow line. She had decided to take the taxi, yet she was pacing forward. She walked over to the edge for no reason and peered below. The memory of the picture surfaced in her mind. She shuddered. She kept on walking, and in front of her lay a little more space to the edge of the platform.

"Stop! What are you doing?" the lean man said.

The next moment, the extra platform, the train, and the lean man disappeared, and Clara fell on the rails. Blackness scattered over her eyes, and she struggled to keep her eyes open. Almost out of the blue, she saw the train advancing towards her at full speed and its yellow lights projecting on her.

She went numb. Her head buzzed like she'd taken ten vodka shots. Glancing at the platform, the last thing she saw was the same woman in a blue kimono dress, holding a grocery bag and a camera in her hand. She grinned widely.

~

June 3rd, 2020, 1:00 p.m., Alabama Police Station

Carl was seated at his designated front desk. He was lying parallel to his desk, studded with the bulk of files. His legs were resting on the couch and his back slumped on the comfortable chair. He didn't expect to attend people since the cases had stopped coming during the lockdown. Even the criminals dreaded going out since none of them wanted to put their life at stake. Last time, when Sam had visited to file the disappearance of Karen, Carl mistook him for a regret- ridden confessor of a small crime.

The boy turned out to be an unconventional eyewitness of a disappearance. Carl half believed and half doubted the boy's story. He didn't believe in the uncanny. All this time, he kept contemplating that the disappearances were carried out by a kidnapping group that was once rooted in the 2000s. He fathomed that they had emerged again. The FBI had given up since there was no proof to be found. He was familiar with the vampire tale and the battle of Trinix but wouldn't take it seriously.

Only a fraction of humans participated in the battle between vampires and homo sapiens, so half the population didn't believe it. He was half of that population until Sam broke into his police station. Laura put an end to the little suspicion he had relevant to their existence. He was at peace, sitting in his comfortable chair, expecting no cases related whatsoever till the lockdown prevailed and the lean man limped to his place.

"Sir," he said, tapping on his desk to command his attention.

"Yes!" Carl, who had his eyes closed, opened it. He studied the man standing in front of him. The lean man was hardly in his forties. He looked weary and concerned. His eyes exhibited fear as if he'd gone through hell and come back alive.

"Sir," he hesitated. "I witnessed the unbelievable!" His demeanor demonstrated a weird kind of panic and urgency. He looked like someone who had just run from a mental asylum.

"Okay…" Carl let out. "Just relax. Have a seat."

The man did as he was told. He sat across from Carl and couldn't stop shivering. "Sorry, sir. But I'm not in a stable state of mind right now," he stammered.

"It's okay," Carl tried to relax him. He was too surprised himself. He nudged the glass of water forward to him. "Here, sip it down."

The man held the glass and took one long swig. "I saw something… something very disturbing. I didn't know whom to reach out − the police station or the psychologist."

"Relax. That'll be decided once you tell me what have you seen?" Carl encouraged the lean man to speak. "What's your good name, by the way?"

"Samuel Patrick," he weakly said.

"Nice name," Carl smiled. "So, Samuel. What did you see? Please enlighten me."

"I'm sitting at the counter of Alabama subway station. Been working there for fifteen years. Yesterday night, a girl dressed in her formal attire came to the station and asked for the next train. I told her so. She waited and slept on the seat. She kept screaming badly in sleep. I came to her and tried waking her up for five minutes, but she didn't until later. She woke up with a shriek and told me that she must have had a nightmare. Just then, on hearing the horns of the train, she walked over to the edge of the platform and fell on the rails. I called out to her. I even gave her my hand to climb up the platform, but she acted like she didn't see it." Samuel took the glass of water and gulped down the rest of the water.

"Well," Carl said. "Suicide is common at the subways and railway stations. I think this was your first time to witness such a thing." He leaned forward on his chair. "I'll suggest you visit the doctor. It might be the trauma of what you witnessed."

"I'm not done yet, sir," Samuel said. He looked as if he would cry any moment now. "She didn't take my hand. Instead, her eyes kept tossing between the approaching train and the woman standing beside me, who was taking her picture. I almost scolded this lady, telling her to stop shooting and focus on helping. This lady grinned at me; her teeth were dripping blood. Run for your life, shaggy. I got scared," he swallowed hard. "And I ran."

Carl was listening intently to this man. He fathomed, "Perhaps, it isn't that much of a suicide case. Please go on. Where did you hide then? What this lady looked like?"

"It is more of a case of unearthly superpowers," Samuel mouthed. "I ran back to my counter and collected my phone, wallet, and coat. I hurried outside the station. One last glance over my shoulder froze me to no end. The train had crushed the girl. This kimono woman was now on the rails, gulping down the remnant flesh of the poor girl. This lady was a beast or a magician. A ghost or a vampire. I don't know." He grew restless.

"Vampire?" Carl said and lost deep in thought.

VampTown

A group of five friends chanted and hooted over their friend's chase. Sara flew back to the VampTown after giving her best at scaring the prey before munching down on her meat. Her friends at the VampTown were watching her scary attempt from a big screen.

"That is by far the scariest attempt ever," Luna marveled. "And sexy too," Miles winked.

"That was hands down, bravo! This mic drop prize money is yours too," Robert said. "What a gem!"

"Yay. I'm going to be Richie Rich," Sara said, giving each of her friends a high-five. Little did she know that she had contracted COVID-19 from Clara, who, in turn, had bought it from her department head. She was a carrier now.

~

June 3, 2020, 11:00 a.m.

Carl started working on his case from scratch, the case that he'd been taking too lightly until yet. He conducted a thorough analysis of the girls and boys who went missing and recorded their time of disappearance. He visited the places where the victims went missing. He dug down the history and read the details related to the battle of Trinix. Slowly but ultimately, he started suspecting the incidences associated with the nocturnal presence. He even recalled how the families of the kidnapped (if they were) had reacted to the news of their loved one's disappearance. The same day, it occurred to Carl how indifferent Laura − the grandmother of Karen, had responded to the news of her granddaughter's disappearance. He called Sam once again and heard about what he had witnessed that day – more carefully this time. With that, he developed the little suspects. If even a tiny lot of what Sam told me had the element of truth to it, it would be easier to get easier for me to track down the nocturnal creatures and stop the disappearances, he thought. The same day, he went over to Laura's place.

8:00 p.m., June 5, 2020

Sophia had made it a routine to come over to Laura's place, use Karen's PC, and try running codes to unlock the vampires' network. Each day she'd come too close to unlocking the unexpected but fail last moment. The site and network security were now a lot more than it was previously. She didn't give up. She kept coming to push her luck and try getting her friend back. More than anything, she was concerned about her security. Laura would come into the room at intervals to ask how successful she'd been in her attempts. She even brought juice and food for her from time to time. That day when she was in the room with her asking about the progress, the doorbell rang. She rose and went to attend the door, thinking about who it could be.

"Hello, Ms. Laura," Carl said. "Mind if I come in?"

Laura was shocked and slightly scared. She took a while to say, "Sure. Get in."

"Getting down to business," Carl stated matter-of-factly. "May I please check the PC Karen owns? I have suspected that she had accidentally entered the wrong network and fallen trap to it."

Laura hesitated. She didn't want Carl to know that Sophia was in there doing the same. "I think it's not the right time for you to break into my house and ask me to use the private devices of my granddaughter. She's a girl; she may have pictures or stuff stored that you shouldn't see."

"But it's important," Carl pressed. "I may help you find your granddaughter."

"She'll return by herself; I'm too sure, inspector," Laura retorted. "Also, I can't allow anyone to use her room, let alone her personal computer. She would be very upset."

"Okay," Carl stood up. "If that's the case." He walked towards the exit when Sophia emerged out of Karen's room and stopped dead upon finding Carl standing in the living room.

Carl tossed glances between the guilty faces of Laura and Sophia and smirked. "Well, I'll think I'll discover the truth for myself now."

He barged into Karen's room, noted the credentials of her searches and network, and left Laura's place. He gave the essential details to the best software engineers in the city and commanded them to track the spooky network and find the vampire's whereabouts based on it. In about a week, he discovered not only the site but also deduced that it was the vampires who took Karen and all the other girls away.

CHAPTER II
ORDERS OF WAR

Carl discussed his findings with the police head constable, who called a meeting with upper subordinates and senior officers in command. Carl reported to them about the prevalent conditions of the country as well as the number of disappearances recorded for the last two months. The Director-General of Police instituted an emergency in the country in response to the frequent nocturnal occurrences and set a curfew in the wake of both possible threats to one's life. Carl was promoted to the reputed position of Senior Police Constable following his outstanding research and survey on the case. He had a troop of twelve policemen to accompany him to places where the incidents occur one after another. He was sure it was the vampires. Every other episode pointed towards it, yet something was missing. Even though he had discovered the vampire rave site, he couldn't track the whereabouts of the beasts that keep landing in their city and quenching their thirst with the inhabitants' blood. The site had its security tight and GPS location concealed. The only thing stopping them from reaching out to the nocturnal creatures was their unseen and intangible whereabouts. Little did he know that not the expert software engineers but a geeky vampire himself would lend them signs to follow.

The VampTown was witnessing equally worse situations than the ones in Alabama city. The death toll of elders resulting from COVID-19 was rising, and the number of young patients recorded was continuously increasing. It was even assumed that younger ones were bringing the disease to the VampTown by consuming the blood of the affected and transmitting the virus monster to their elders. The government officials forwarded the orders of lockdown and instructed everyone to avoid landing down on human land and consuming their blood. Instead, they were requested to have deer's blood, which was a lot healthier and can quickly be delivered to their doorsteps on one call. Despite that, the younger lot at VampTown had their taste buds developed; they couldn't resist the urge to have the junk blood of humans. They only consumed deer's blood during sickness. The youngsters, reckless and irresponsible, bore no ear to the COVID-19 precautions and preventive guidelines. They continued with their hunt down the city and brought the same germs over and over again due to their temptations. At the same time, some younger and careless lot in Alabama City also couldn't keep themselves from going out either, especially the ones with daily wages or other needs. One such person was Alby, her best friend, Sheena's birthday was near. She had to go to the gift shop and purchase something for herself. Earlier, Sheena had left no stone unturned to shower her with presents and make her day. It was her turn then. Her brother, Michael, dropped her at the gift shop on his way to the office – an emergency meeting was called at 7:00 p.m. – now she had to return home on her own. That wasn't a big deal. She was habitual of taking the double-decker. Thankfully, it was operational during the lockdown as well. So, what if it wasn't stacked with many passengers like the way it used to be before the lockdown? At least it was following the same routes and was open for passengers' conveyance. After purchasing the gifts, she emerged out of the bright lights of the gift shop and mingled with the darkness. To her gratitude, she didn't have to wait long before the double-decker arrived and took her in. She took the last seat. The vehicle had hardly moved a minute or two before it halted to take in another passenger. This man dressed in blue jeans and a yellow jacket had his hoodie up covering his face. He climbed up the decker with a parcel and squandered as if he were drunk. He secured his place right ahead of Alby, put the parcel down next to him, and tilted his head. Soon, his loud snores were the only sound audible on the bus. "Weirdo!" Alby whispered. "What an odd way to sleep!"

His snores got louder. Alby put her headphones on, but she could still hear the thundering snores. She took them off in anger and put them back in her bag. A few seconds later, this man fell face-first onto the floor. Quite amusingly, his streaks of snores continued despite the fall. The very next minute, he started sleepwalking. Alby looked over at him in shock as he marched up and down the bus. Suddenly, he stopped and sat beside her.

A cold shiver ran down her spine. She tried to ebb away from the man, but he inched closer. "Ahhh…" he mouthed; his breath smelled like a rotten egg. It was disgusting to the extent that Alby fell unconscious. The moment she woke up, there was no one on the bus. This ugly stranger was gone. As she moved to rise, she felt the sting on her left arm. She looked down to see what was hurting this bad and found a red sprout planted on her arm. The blood was dripping down from it.

She went over to the bus driver and requested him to drop her at a nearby hospital. The driver was friendly and did the same. Stopping by the hospital, she felt as if her energy was draining. With much difficulty, she managed to tread inside the hospital and reach the doctor. She showed the red sprout to the doctor and fainted on the chair after feeling another bout of fatigue.

She remained unconscious for the next three days. The doctors observed weird patterns and how her health began degenerating day by day. Her skin got more pale, weary, and loose, and her condition got worse. More than anything, the doctors had their focus on the red tree-pattern sprout that dripped blood twice over the night. Alby's blood count was going down rapidly. Every day 500cc of blood was transfused into her body due to the sudden unexpected drop. Five days later, one of the doctors found the cause and called Carl, deeming it a police case.

When Carl arrived, the same doctor showed him the tree-pattern tattoo on his arm of Alby and informed him, "This is insane!" he paused. "We haven't received a case like this before. The patient fainted before telling us how she got the tattoo. But this tree-pattern thing," he stammered, "I presume, is a bloodsucker. Someone is feeding on her blood through this tattoo. Pardon me if I sound drunk, but I'm not. She's losing 100cc of blood twice a day. It's beyond what her body can produce. We're transfusing just enough blood for her to survive."

Carl looked closely at the tattoo. "Someone just can't consume the blood without having software helping him do so." "Whoever it is," he paused, "might be in desperate need of blood daily. Didn't know that humans could go to this extreme to suck the life out of someone just to have theirs." "Doesn't appear like the human's attempt," Carl said, scanning the tattoo. "What is the solution to this?" he inquired.

"We have to amputate the arm from the shoulder to take it out. Its roots are long, or in the next five days, the beast will take away 2/3 part of her body," the doctor informed. "Have you discussed it with her family or her?" Carl sounded concerned. "Yeah. First thing," the doctor replied. "It was hard for them to digest. They don't know either what's happening, but they permitted us to do so. Also, there are no chances of Alby waking up until we remove the arm." "Alright," Carl sighed. "That's very sad." He fell again on the red-sprouted tree on her arm with dried blood.

"By the way, when are you planning to perform the amputation?" Carl asked.

"Tomorrow, noon," the doctor said.

"Would you mind if I have my team of network trackers around the night?" Carl gently requested. "We need to get to the person who planted the tattoo.

Could you also inform me of the timings when the blood-sucking is carried out?"

"Of course not. I won't mind. Bring in your men if they can track out the criminal. Also, I'm not sure of the timings, but it's done overnight, that I can guarantee you," the doctor was confident.

"No problem. My network trackers will find it out." Carl extended his hand out. "Thank you so much, doctor. This information is going to be a great help if it is what I assume it is."

"What do you think it is?" The doctor questioned.

"You'll get to know it soon," Carl smiled and left. He sent his team of expert network trackers, two of whom were inside the ward, and the other two were outside.

Meanwhile, a team of web tracking experts had been keeping an eye on the vampire rave site, more specifically on the activity of Karen's account. There were no other accounts of girls and boys who went missing earlier. Also, no one witnessed their disappearance except for Sam, who watched the unseen. The web trackers were vigilant, checking movements, logins, or not even the slightest bit of activity, but there wasn't anything. They went over all the previous activity logs of Karen and found videos, posts, conversations, and pictures, and communicated every detail to Carl. The only thing they couldn't grasp was the last video call made by Cancer to invite Karen to their land. In eager pursuit of looking for activity, they finally tracked one from Karen's vampire rave account.

Karen felt a wave of depression running down her bones. She recalled the great times of the last month when she discovered the vampire's site for the first time and suddenly felt associated with the vampire family. She reflected on the visual of a month when she shared her video, got appreciation, and felt connected with them. For the first time in her life, she felt the need to share her singing video, never had she once sung before in school or college. Only Laura and Sophia were aware of her singing talent, but she didn't display her gift in front of the audience. As a child, she always dreamed of becoming a singer. Instead of toys, she saved money to buy herself a guitar and had been playing it since. She wasn't familiar with such love, recognition, and respect before. The people at the vampire rave site made her feel welcome and treated her like family. She never felt like an outcast, which was one reason why she opened up to them the way she never did in her school. An overwhelming gripped her over the thought of how she had disappointed the vampires by hiding her true identity and pretending to be a part of them. She got all the love, respect, and attention, but she felt like she didn't know how to handle that and ended up ruining everything. "Ouch," she sat up. Her body was aching. She lifted her hand, which felt ten pounds heavier and grabbed the phone from the side table. She contemplated doing what she was about to do and turned the cell phone. She wasn't concerned about her safety or dreaded being tracked by the vampires to have her blood. She didn't fear death and had always been dauntless, but the only thing she couldn't live with was regret. She felt an insurmountable need to make her confessions, state her remorse, and extend her apology. Overcome by her feelings, she followed her instincts. Posting the camera at just the right angle, she started shooting herself.

"Hello, Vami-tooth," she sighed. "I don't know where to start. There is a multitude of feelings, emotions, and sentiments going on inside of me. I'll begin with the truth. Yes, I am a warm-blooded human, and I hid this secret from all of you. Down in Alabama City, while I was preparing my project of network tracking, I bumped into the site and found nocturnal activity. You can thank God that it was me." She sipped from the glass of water and continued. "Here at Alabama City, I never felt accepted due to my nocturnal routine. Me and granny, Laura, and Goth descendants. We are alone in our town. We cannot mingle with humans due to our peculiar way of doing things, also because we look up to vampires." She giggled. "You must be thinking, why would a human, let alone a Goth descendant, be so inspired by vampires?"

"Well. Laura and I still have our loyalties to Lord Byron, who saved us in the Battle of Trinix. My parent, Bella, and James died fighting the same war." She paused.

"This is not the first time I've come to VampTown. I've been here in my childhood after the war because of the threats to our life by humans who could've killed us for supporting vampires if we lived down in Alabama City. Laura and I resided in VampTown for a bit until the weather conditions and suitable recourse to nourishment made it difficult for us to stay healthy. Lord Byron sent us down and wiped the memory of half the residents so we could live there in peace."

Just then, Zobray entered her room. He beamed at her, and she smiled back. Watching her shooting the video, he sat on the bed opposite her and didn't mouth a word. Zobray was sick. He had contracted Covid-19 from Karen and was quarantined in his room. The only time he'd come to her was at night to give some bread, carrot soup, and a cookie. He'd even keep some spare dry food like chips, biscuits, and cereal for Karen to have in the daytime if she, by chance, woke up. Karen would eagerly wait for the clock to strike nine because it was the only time of the day when she had company and finally got to see him. The walls of the room, otherwise, seemed to cave in on her and slump her inside her head.

"For the first time as I logged into the Vampire Rave account, I felt like I'd returned home. I started singing, laughing, and talking to people. Never I have before felt so loved, appreciated, and accepted by people like the way I did simply by sharing one song. I thought I'd finally found my family; my people and I couldn't wait to come here. Cancer warmly invited me here, telling me that you all were eagerly waiting to see me perform, but I guess I ruined everything. I disappointed you all." She sighed. "Perhaps, I don't deserve a family. Once an outcast forever, an outcast. I'm going back home since I don't want to give your patience a hard time or compel you to control your urges. Even if half of you decide to stop by and consume my blood, you will be more than welcome to do so. But if I get the chance to return alive to my town, I'll still protect your secret with my life. Anything for the loyalty; anything for the honor. See you."

Karen saves the video and shares it on her profile. She turns the device off and glances up at Zobray, who looked concerned.

"Are you leaving?"

"Yes, probably tonight at 4:00 a.m. I'll speak with Cancer; I'm sure he won't force me to stay," Karen said.

"Won't you miss me, Karen?" For the first time, Zobray's expressions were dead serious. Karen had otherwise only seen him jovial, energetic, and full of life.

She giggled. "Of course, I will." She came forward and took his hand in hers. "I've troubled you a lot, Zobray. You've done so much for me and what I did. I paid you back by transmitting my disease to you. I don't deserve a friend like you."

"It's not like that, Karen," Zobray defended. "I enjoyed spending time with you. I –"

"I'm a disappointment, Zobray," Karen interjected. "I'm good for nothing. I don't deserve anything," her voice was brittle. "I ruined the little love I received from the people here. I don't deserve love eith –"

Zobray quickly put his lips on hers. He kissed her, synchronically, the upper lip, then the lower one. Karen felt his warm lips against hers as he planted gentle kisses. In five seconds, he pulled back.

"I want you to consider my proposal, Karen," Zobray stated, looking intently at her. "It wasn't a joke when I said I wanted to continue the legacy of my parents by doing the human-vampire reunion." His eyes were pleading. "I would have still suspected the possibility if I hadn't met you. I fell for you the moment I saw you."

Karen was quiet. She struggled to speak but couldn't find the right words. Her brain sent messages that went fuzzy soon as the desires of her body crept in. The past few weeks had been very exhausting, thrusting her down the emotional drain. At this moment, she was giving up what she had been holding for so long.

Abruptly and quite suddenly, she leaped towards him and mingled her lips with his. Zobray wrapped his arms around her back and kissed her hard. Their warm foreheads met, and their noses scrunched against each other as they kept their lips busy. The next second, Zobray ripped off her shirt, whose buttons fell off as he did. She pulled off his shirt quickly. They had a weird urgency of a magnet with opposite poles, notwithstanding being apart at this moment. He gave mouth-open kisses from her neck, shoulders then down to her chest and belly like a hungry wolf. Karen moaned. He took off her jeans and then his. The next moment, they met and made love to their satisfaction.

Soon, as they parted, Zobray kissed her forehead. "I came here to tell you that we have an appointment today at 11:00 p.m. Do get ready, love."

Fifteen minutes later, they got ready and set off to the doctor's place on foot. The night was dark and inviting. Karen wasn't afraid since she had Zobray along, also now that she had spoken her mind in the video. Nothing else would bother her now, even if someone stopped by and decided to suck her blood.

Halfway on their route to the hospital, they stopped to rest. They sat in the garden underneath a massive building on the edge of which a sick bat was sitting. It was a vampire whose body was gelled with the gooey serum. This vampire had Covid-19. He continuously secreted gooey serum and dripped it on the ground.

"By the way," Zobray grinned. "I'm the only lucky vampire who got the honor of tasting you," he winked.

Karen laughed hard. "Lucky you!" she said. Just when she was laughing mouth open, something dropped from her mouth down to her throat. Her eyes shot wide open.

"What was that?" she let out and struggled to puke. Too late. She sensed a buzz of energy inside her body and fainted.

A meeting was called out again by the Director-General of Police with his subordinates and officers after he was informed about the video shared by Karen.

"She's alive," the DCOP said. "That's the big news."

"And a Goth descendant too," the Deputy DCOP added.

"She and her granny also have their loyalties with the vampires," a senior subordinate joined in.

"On top of it all off, she'd been to VampTown before, which is to say, this Gothic family was left out when we were wiping out the entire Goth and vampire army from our planet."

"It's strange how they managed to survive," a police constable added. "Though they're only women."

"The question is what to do now," Carl finally said. "She's coming back, at least that's what the video message suggests. What should be done to her for having her loyalties with the enemy?"

"We'll get to that once she comes," the DCOP stated matter-of-factly. "Just tell me, did you follow the orders concerning Laura?"

"Yes, sir," Carl informed. "I sent my team to her place. She is arrested and interrogated. But we can't do much in her case since she's a madwoman – people say. The court will set her free immediately upon declaring her mental condition unstable. We need to reach out to Karen in any way."

"What report your network trackers at the hospital have put across so far?" the DCOP inquired.

"They're on it. Any activity or network, and they'll inform me," Carl enlightened.

"Okay," the DCOP said and turned to look over the rest of the men. "So, what's the next mode of action? How do you think these vampires are going to stop?"

"I can't think of anything right now when we don't have any clue in hand or details related to their whereabouts," the Deputy DCOP surrendered.

The rest of them bowed their heads in surrender too, giving it a slight shake as their brains couldn't lend them any idea.

Just then, Carl's mobile buzzed. He looked over at the message, and a broad smile sketched across his face.

DCOP's eyes fell on him, and he immediately questioned him.

"You are not in your living room, Carl. Put your phone down," he commanded. "Propose the idea if you have any?"

"Sir," Carl started, a smile affixed on his face. "Good

news! Our team of expert network trackers has tracked out the location of vampires. It's called VampTown."

"That's great news! Where are they located?" the DCOP was beaming.

"A smart location," Carl frowned. "A route which even the pilots don't take."

"Well, let's begin with the teasing then," the Governor of Alabama City said, standing at the door. Everyone stood up from their seat. "Settle down, everyone."

"Perfect timing, sir," the DCOP smiled. "Also, the command was taken."

"Yes," the governor secured his place on the round table. "We'll tease them first, just as they began by kidnapping our people," he sipped down from the glass of water. "Gear up for Battle of Trinix II, my men!"

CHAPTER 12
UNITED YET SO APART

Ten years ago.

"Dear child," Lord Byron weakly said. His breath was raspy and brittle. He was lying on his back, knowing that he might breathe his last any moment now. For this reason, he started warning his grandson of the coming times. "I've lived my life, took things in stride, and survived it all with power, patience, and sometimes wits," he paused to cough.

Cancer nodded. He was listening very intently to what his grandfather was struggling to communicate in a low and hoarse voice.

"But my child," he continued. "I must inform you about the coming times when you'll come to power." Cancer was only sixteen then. "Ten years from now, at twenty-six years of age, you'll have the reign over the whole of VampTown. You'll be loved, respected, and followed for life if you stay wise."

"I will," Cancer assured him, taking his weak hands in his. "Don't worry, Grandpa."

"Dear," Byron said and had difficulty swallowing down the saliva in his mouth. "The reign wouldn't be a cup of tea given the animosity we've borne with the warm-blooded species. Though half of them believe that we were finished in the Battle of Trinix, the other half still think that we fled. For this reason, your generation will have to make sure not to tease them in any way and prevent oneself from the urge of consuming their blood, as this could spark a war."

"I'll be careful, Grandpa." Tears dripped down his eyes over the thought of losing his only family—Byron.

"You have to be," he looked into Cancer's eyes. "The hatred of homo sapiens is undeniably intense towards the vampires." Lord Byron turned to face the window and stared at the distance. "I'm having visions, Cancer. And I don't want this to happen to you. The warm-blooded species will try to attack vampires again in an attempt to eradicate the vampire community from this planet. This wouldn't be an overnight decision stemming out of hatred, but rather a consequence of our community's actions. You must preach to your tribe to feed on deer's blood as it is healthier for them. Make sure the vamitooth don't turn up being a victim of their own unhealthy choices."

"I will take care of it, Grandpa."

"Dear," Lord Byron turned and gazed at Cancer. "I can see it coming. The vampires won't listen, I know." He gasped as a look of worry washed over his face, and his shortness of breath took over.

"You okay, Grandpa?" Cancer quickly stood up and covered Lord Byron, both his hands placed on his grandfather's cheeks. He was turning cold.

"I don't have much time," Lord Byron urgently informed. "I just want you to know that your only safe zone in the coming times would be a girl from the Goth tribe. Do I have to mention her name?"

Cancer gave his head a negating shake, thinking that he knew whom his grandpa was referring to here. Also, he couldn't see Lord Byron in pain. The way he was struggling to deliver his words was too painful to watch. Cancer believed that he read his mind. Earlier as well, when he was crying while bidding little Karen farewell, Lord Byron told him not to worry and that she'd be back. Cancer got the gist from there. He still had his doubts and suspicions about finding her again when she broke into a vampire rave site out of the blue and tried to settle in. It was the universe indeed trying to conspire a way of setting up her return to VampTown.

Sitting at his office and watching the video Karen had recently shared on her personal account, Cancer couldn't help but reflect on everything from scratch. He wasn't concerned about his reputation, which would surely be affected owing to the blame he'd receive for bringing a human to VampTown and simultaneously hiding her identity. He was only worried about Karen for the decision she had taken of returning to her city. He couldn't help but feel bad for Karen for how isolated and deprived she had felt despite living in a community of humans. He wished he could keep her in VampTown, but since she had openly revealed her identity and welcomed vampires to have her blood while she'd been on her way to retreat, Cancer couldn't stop her. Part of it was to ensure her safety since he knew vampires could be thirsty for her blood and secondly because he failed her. Badly. Now, even if Karen approached him to tell him she was leaving, he wouldn't be able to stop her because of the threats he'd geared in her direction.

He watched her video and sighed. Silently, he waited for the angry reaction of the vampires and only hoped that none of them would consume her blood. He made a phone call to Zobray.

"Hey, Zobray," he greeted. "What's the report?"

"Boss! I was about to call you!" Zobray informed. "Karen fainted while we were on our way to the hospital; we had our check-up for Covid-19."

"Is this what Corona is doing to the patients now?" Cancer inquired anxiously. "And how are you dealing with the disease so far?"

"Can't say, boss!" Zobray said. "She's a human, after all. Her symptoms might be different from mine," he sighed. "And, I'm fine."

"Okay, Zobray. Just take extra care of her now. The vampires can chase her out now, and you know why. Be more careful. And keep me posted about her progress, okay?"

"Roger!" Zobray said and hung up.

To distract his mind from the stresses, he flipped open the television. The screen displayed one of the vampire movies starring Kirsten Stewart and Robert Pattinson. Notwithstanding anything apart from reality, Cancer changed the channel and landed on a news telecast. Broadcasting the news was a cute, dimpled girl in a baggy white top, an over-worn black coat, and black jeans. Cancer amplified the volume to hear what she had to say.

"...Karen has also claimed that she has been living as an outcast in Alabama City and has no tribe to call her own. She mingled with the vamitooth because she has her roots associated with VampTown, and she has been there before. On watching the video, the vampires have come out of their house—"

Cancer rubbed his eyes; his suspicion was now becoming a reality. Fear gripped him on hearing the last words of the news telecaster.

"The vampires will eat her alive," he mouthed to himself and picked up his phone to call Zobray.

"...Yes! This is true. They've come out of their house, not in the thirst of consuming her blood but to show their support. To own her as a vamitooth. As you can see in the live feed," the screen quickly switched and showed the live coverage of people gathered in a big horde, roaring and hooting.

"Karen—we love you!"

"Karen, you are one of us."

"We want you to stay, melody queen."

Cancer couldn't believe his eyes. A moment later, his eyes welled up over the heartwarming support. Never had he felt so proud of his people. An insane wave of courage and confidence settled over him, and he now knew how to stop Karen even if she decided to leave.

He puffed out a satisfactory sigh and slumped back in his seat to take a quick nap. Just then, Lazarus emerged into his room and demanded his urgent attention.

"Cancer!" he called out. "Are you up?"

"Yeah!" Cancer's eyes snapped open upon hearing the panicky and slightly raspy voice of Lazarus. "Yes, I am. All okay?"

"Not really," Lazarus said as he walked into the room and took a seat across the table. "Another intruder network has tried reaching us out."

"What?" Cancer bolted up. "Who could it be now?"

"I don't know," Lazarus wiped the beads of sweat on his forehead. "And it isn't through the vampire rave site. It's from another source that our engineers are working on."

"I wonder who it could be," Cancer absentmindedly looked at the silver paperweight on his table.

There was another knock on the door, and Ricinus stepped in.

"Sir," he gazed directly at Cancer. "Someone from the intruder's network wants to speak to you."

Cancer exchanged a worrisome glance with Lazarus and shot up quickly. He hurried to the working station and watched the big screen, starring four people who were staring back at him as he walked into the networking department.

The strangers on the screen were sitting in a close circle as if about to have a round-table conference. The man sitting in the middle was dressed in a grey suit, white shirt, and red tie. He had a boastful grin on his face as he stared at Cancer coming in. Sitting on his left was Carl in his uniform, and to his right were two broad men with stern faces.

"Whoa!" the governor who was seated in the middle rejoiced. "Why do vampires look exactly like humans?" he sneered.

Cancer read the overconfident face of this man and sat a meter or two away from the screen for them to have a clearer view of the two.

"Or more handsome, you can say," Cancer joked sarcastically. "Anyways, gentlemen, may I know your names and ask how you got to us?"

The governor passed a mocking smile at Cancer and gestured to Carl to speak as if he was saving his words for later yet better purposes.

"Well," Carl began. "I'm the Senior Police Constable from Alabama City."

"Director General of Police, Paul Hemistich," informed a stern-faced man in his late forties.

"Deputy Director General of Police, Truman Abbot," a fat, thick-mustached man introduced himself. He tried to put on an angry face but failed to display a flinty demeanor. None paid heed to him.

"And you?" Cancer inquired, pointing at the man in the middle.

The Governor smirked at the flat disposition of courage and confidence by Cancer. He did not speak and nudged Carl to speak on his behalf.

"Well, I must request you to address Mr. Salvador Maison with respect," Carl warned. "He's the State Governor of Alabama City and is here to discuss a serious matter of consideration."

"That's okay," Salvador said. "We're not here to win hearts or make relationships with these nocturnal creatures. I don't demand their respect for a brief period. After all, by the end of this conversation, they'll automatically respect me or hate me." He smirked at Carl, and then while addressing the two people in front of him on the screen, he continued, "We're just here for some time and will leave after doing the necessary." He paused. "You two can also introduce yourselves so we can get down to business."

"Alright," Cancer leaned forward and introduced

himself confidently. Lazarus did the same. "Now speaking of business, how did you get to us?"

"Well, it's a very long story," Carl said, pulling open the thick stack of a file before him on the table. "However, we'll get to that."

"Go on, tell me precisely," Cancer demanded.

Carl glanced up from his file and grinned, "I must appreciate the confidence. I'm just too sure it won't be there after a while." He landed on a page and stopped. "Well, Mr. Cancer. You must be well aware of Alabama City and have information related to where it is located?"

Cancer gazed dead in the eyes of Carl and convincingly said, "No. Where is it?"

"Hahaha… well, in that case, you must ask your tribe!" Carl snorted. "They enjoy hunting down here for midnight muse."

"I don't get it what you're —"

Cancer was interjected as Carl began narrating the disappearances recorded in the past six months. "Sia. She was last seen in the Dixon club attending her college's Halloween party. Mia — who went missing after getting into the thick of Conecuh Forest, following the rare thunder strikes," Carl glanced up to look for

Cancer's expression to check for any sign of worry, but he displayed none. "Following the thunder strikes and a painful wail of the deer, as reported by her husband, Miles. Olivia – who disappeared in Dixon street never to be found and Karen…" he paused. "By the way, how's Karen doing? Are you guys taking good care of her?"

"She's doing quite well here, thank you," Cancer retorted. "You continue."

"Well, I can see that for myself in the latest video she'd shared on her personal account," Carl riposted.

Cancer was shocked. He exchanged a worrisome glance with Lazarus as they both realized that their network was constantly being tracked by a group of hackers on earth. They said nothing and listened quietly in anticipation of what the four humans were going to say next.

"One of her college boys, Sam, watched Karen disappearing out of sight right before his eyes in the forest of Conecuh." Carl read out. "He even claimed to have seen a weird creature in a black hoodie watching over Karen as she did so and warned him to run away from that place." Carl delved out of his file and asked, "Who do you think this man could be, Mr. Cancer? Who could be this protective of Karen?"

Lazarus looked sideways at Cancer, who had his eyes affixed on Carl. He swallowed down a lump in his throat and yet mouthed, "Please get to the point, Mr. Carl."

"Well," Carl continued. "Then there was Alex, the only boy whose death was recorded. Guess one of your gay men has an appetite for men. Makes sense, anyways. And then Clara, who was thrown off the tracks by a girl in a kimono dress. There was an eyewitness too who reported about how this pale-white human-like creature fed on her remnants. And, Alby…" Carl closed the file in his hands. "One network and programming expert of yours has been successfully sucking on Alby's blood via a tree-pattern tattoo that was planted on her left arm. It is through his weak data system that the whereabouts of your VampTown have been tracked. Could you please tell this person of yours to stop doing that because this girl is losing blood down here at intervals."

"Okay," Cancer said. "Well, you're right. All these activities were carried out by the inhabitants of VampTown. What next? Are you going to chase us out? Try your luck with that. And we aren't returning Karen to your place. This is for sure."

"Whoa! We have chased you out, boy," Salvador said. "We are just here to ask for confessions and a promise of no repetition of the previous deeds. Or you must get ready for worse."

"Worse? Really?" Cancer said. "Well, try out worse first, and then we'll think about promises of no repetition."

"You sure?" Salvador smirked.

"Damn sure…" Cancer mouthed. He wanted to witness their power and see for himself how much they tracked them out.

"Well, no glimpses then," Salvador said. "Here begins the first teasing before the Battle of Trinix II."

With that, thunder blew, and the whole of VampTown shook to its beatings. It almost felt like an earthquake. The firm ground of the cloud crumbled and thudded like a heartbeat.

"Goodbye for now!" Salvador smirked. "Hope you'll love the first teaser after your six months of blood-thirsty teasers."

Half an hour later, as the mud and the shaky ground settled, Cancer got to know that an air jet had glided past their region and hit one of the buildings.

The next day, Karen visited Cancer and informed him about her quick restoration to health.

"My God," Cancer mouthed. "I can't believe you're

perfectly fine. I just watched you on a live call a day ago, and you were pale and weak. Look at you now!" he gasped.

"I'm perfectly fine, and I've found the formula to survive Covid-19. Zobray told me everything about your conversation with Mr. Salvador and what sparked the attack." She paused. "Please allow me to speak to him as I can settle the dispute."

"But…" Cancer had questions about what Karen was about to discuss.

"Please trust me, Cancer," she stated with conviction. "And stay with me during the conversation."

Ricinus connected to the same network and arranged the phone call to which Carl and the DDCOP responded.

"Hello," Karen said. "Hope you two are doing well."

"Hi," Carl grinned, confusing this call as the one for surrender. "We're doing very well." He paused as he studied Karen's face. "You look very fresh and healthy. What's the secret?"

"Happiness and thoughts of peace," Karen mocked back.

"Whoa! Shall we count this as a message of surrender then?" the DDCOP sarcastically inquired.

"Not exactly," Karen answered. "But a middle way out. A deal!"

"Go on!" Carl mouthed.

"Well," she began, "I contracted Coronavirus while I was in Alabama City, and the symptoms began to appear while I resided in VampTown. I was the only human yet equally contagious for vampires if they decided to consume my blood or stick around. Fortunately, I was safe, but my proximity to someone infected him. It wasn't until I stepped out of my house to head for the hospital when a gooey serum accidentally fell on my mouth, and I recovered from this virus."

"Bullshit!" the DDCOP mouthed. "I don't believe you."

"This is true," Karen responded curtly. "Moreover, the boy who planted a tree-pattern tattoo on Alby's shoulder was a Covid-19 positive patient and was looking for his sustenance while staying at home. That is one reason he thought of this way and kept sucking on the blood of Alby—the healthy person—and recovered from this disease."

Cancer was watching Karen in awe. He was also listening to these details for the very first time. He glanced up at Zobray for confirmation, who, in return, gave him a quiet nod of approval.

"Vampires possess the power to cure humans through the gooey serum they secrete. In the same way, one sip of a healthy person's blood can cure the infected vampires. We are the cure for one another if we clear our heads of hatred and think straight. Battles can't cure anything, and even if they can, then we can fight it later since none of us are going anywhere. Better think about fighting the pandemic that has already taken thousands of humans' and vampires' lives. The choice is yours!"

CHAPTER 13

UNISON

"Hello, old lady," said a stern-faced, manly-voiced lady in a dark blue uniform. A small, rectangular nameplate on her chest read, Terresa Wales.

Laura opened her saggy eyes and struggled to see clearly. A woman, with a glass of water in her hand, was cowering over her. Laura felt the hardwood chair beneath her on which she'd been seated for an hour now. Her head was resting on the table before her. She was in a four-walled room. There was a bright lamp hanging above her head, bright enough to coerce squints without directly looking at it. Laura was squinting, struggling to take in the details of the room she was in. It was an investigation cell, and she was being inquired about.

Suddenly, Terresa splashed the water on her face. "Get up, old lady! We don't have all day."

"I told you everything I know," Laura stammered.

"That you don't know where your granddaughter is? Bullshit!" Terresa came closer, her face close to Laura's. She locked her fingers in Laura's hair and pulled. "Tell me now, how else have you and Karen been supporting the vampires in their foul affairs? Are you involved in the disappearance of other girls in Alabama?"

"You are mistaken, woman," Laura let out weak blinks. "We are not a part of it. We lead our normal lives and harm no one."

"Don't play out this innocence in front of me. I know you've attended the Battle of Trinix and had your loyalty to the Vampires. I even know that you've been to VampTown in your life. It is no secret that your granddaughter is still there, telling us tales of how well she is being kept there."

"I don't know what you're saying," Laura mouthed amid shaky breaths. "I don't remember anything."

"Well, you sure do!" Terresa retorted. "But you are of no good use to us. Now you will call Karen back in Alabama."

"I'll not!" Laura said hoarsely.

"Well, you'll have to." Terresa clenched two fingers of Laura's between the pen and pulled them back.

"Ouch!" Laura groaned in pain. "I'm not calling my granddaughter here if she has trouble awaiting her."

"She should have thought that before calling for trouble," Terresa grinned. She picked up her phone and opened the video camera. "Quick now! Call Karen back."

"I won't," Laura breathed. Her eyes were hardly opening as she spoke.

"Alright now," Terresa stood up and fetched a machine from another. "Speak up, or you'll be electrocuted."

"I won't," Laura cried. Her eyes were revealing horrors.

"Okay then." Terresa placed the machine on her head. "On the count of three. Three."

"No way!" Laura stubbornly said.

"Two."

Laura shook her head in disapproval.

"One!"

"Never!" Laura gritted furiously. Terresa pressed the red switch.

"Karen!!!" Laura screamed.

"Granny!" Karen shrieked and woke up in her bed. She fumbled on the side table for a glass of water and tripped it. Mindlessly, she got up, and some broken shards pierced her skin. The blood began to drip out.

Upon hearing the unexpected crushing sound from Karen's room, Zobray, who was awake in his room, woke up and dropped in. He watched Karen sitting on the bed and groaning in pain as she pulled out the glass shards from her feet. He dashed forth in her direction, and a delicious smell of pure honey blood infused his senses. Karen watched in horror as Zobray's expressions changed, and he appeared as if he was about to lose his control.

Zobray got up and got the mop from the washroom in her room. He swabbed the floor clean of the little pool of blood and washed the mop in the washroom. Coming outside, he glanced at Karen's feet weakly and met her eyes. She looked worried now. Zobray walked up to the dresser and grabbed the first aid kit from the first drawer.

He walked around the bed and took his place on the floor, near her feet. He observed some shards that were still stabbed into her feet. He put the first aid kit aside, took the cotton, soaked it in water, and wiped her feet clean of the blood. He glanced up to meet her eyes, weakness evident in his own, and gently pulled two of the glass remnants from her feet. As he did, blood came spurting out. He quickly put his mouth on the open wound and sucked the blood for as long as it dripped. He glanced up and weakly met the terror-ridden eyes of Karen.

"Don't worry. I'll never do you wrong." He took the bandage and wrapped it around her feet. Karen leaned forward and gave him a gentle peck on the lips.

"Is everything okay?" Zobray asked as she pulled back to wipe the tears from her eyes.

"I'm not sensing things right." She had a look of concern on her face. "Granny could be in trouble because of the video I shared. I need to speak with the Governor!" Karen palpitated.

"Hey." Zobray touched his forehead with hers. Their noses scrunched. "Don't worry," he said and thought about his next step.

Evening, 9:00 p.m.

Cancer had his gaze tossing between Karen and Zobray. "I didn't think about it," he finally said. "I was only happy about the fact that you're staying in

VampTown. I almost forgot that you had Laura down there waiting for you."

"I love my granny, and I can do anything in this world for her. Even if it means traveling down to that hell city I've been living in."

Cancer watched Karen while he had his mind looking for solutions. Just then, Lazarus emerged into the room.

"Cancer, the governor and his police team are asking for face time. Guess they've tried our samples of gooey serum on their patients," Lazarus assumed. "Come on now. We must speak to them."

Cancer stood up and looked over at Karen. "Come with me." He offered his hand. Karen looked over her shoulder at Zobray, who nodded with a smile. She took Cancer's hand and followed him to the network department, and a minute later, the face time began.

"Good evening," the governor said. Quite amazingly, this man wasn't exhibiting the pride he exuded earlier in his first face-time. "I hope you all are doing great."

"So we are," Cancer replied. "Let's get it straight. Did you try the sample on your Covid-19 patients?"

"Yes, we did," the governor informed.

"How did it go?" Cancer inquired.

"Very well," the governor said in a state of shock. "Both patients have been cured. It's strange yet amazing."

"That's great," Cancer said with a smile. "What do you suggest now? Shall we start the trade? We'll need healthy blood too, and we have collected enough gooey serum for your people."

"We are on it," the governor replied. "Start the trade. How can we deliver the blood?"

"The same place where we delivered the gooey serum. Conecuh Forest," Cancer suggested. "But before that," he paused and glanced at Karen, "we need a favor so that we can continue with the exchange."

"Okay, and what is it?" the governor replied. Scowls began to appear on her forehead.

"You've seen the video of Karen, right? And you know hers and her granny's true identity now. They are Goths and share a special relationship with vampires. I would only want to know where Laura is at present."

"Yes, we have seen the video, and we are completely aware of their truth. Laura is with our team. She is under interrogation," the governor informed.

"As you know, she has unstable mental health; you can hardly get details out of her. Moreover, I know how badly you want to get rid of Goths from your town," Cancer said.

"Yeah, so?" the governor asked.

"I suggest you set her free and send her to us. She's the last of the Goths left in Alabama City. As for the information you need, you can get that from Karen," Cancer suggested.

The governor exchanged looks with Carl and DCOP. "Give us two minutes to decide."

"Alright," Cancer said. "We're waiting."

The FaceTime went on mute, but the three of them could be seen from the screen, discussing it. Karen gazed hopefully at the senior authority men of Alabama City and looked warmly at Cancer. After three minutes or so, the FaceTime resumed, and the governor looked directly at Karen.

"We are willing to set her free and, at the same time, transport her to your world," the governor paused. "But yes, Karen will have to answer all the questions on her behalf."

"I'll do that!" Karen quickly said. "Thank you so much."

"Could you then bring her to the Conecuh Forest tonight and we'll get her from there?" Cancer asked.

"Not so early," the governor replied. "Not before Karen gives us all the answers."

"Alright, then. What are you waiting for?" Karen questioned.

"One of our investigation experts will have a FaceTime with you," the governor said. "We'll inform you about it." He turned to face Cancer. "By the way, the healthy blood will be delivered to the Conecuh Forest tonight. Grab that after twelve."

Days stretched into weeks, and both the vampires and humans joined hands to save each other's lives. The healthy humans began donating their blood to the vampires, and the nocturnal species started jarring up the gooey serum for the humans. As soon as the remedy was delivered in both regions, Covid-19 began to be eradicated from both places. Karen had her investigative sessions with Terresa. She answered every question of hers correctly. Since Karen was only a child during the first battle and had nothing to do with the hatred, she was steered clear by Terresa. As for Laura, she was already old and not in a stable state of mind; she was easily set free and left in the Conecuh Forest for the vampires to receive her from there.

In this way, things ended on a peaceful note. The

second battle didn't spike because both species saved each other from becoming extinct. At the same time, they left each other with a promise not to disturb each other's lives ever again. Years passed, and the vampires didn't instigate the humans by flying down to feed on their blood. On the other hand, humans and their system changed their air route, never to disturb the vampires again.

www.ingramcontent.com/pod-product-compliance
Lightning Source LLC
Chambersburg PA
CBHW051233130726
47988CB00001B/337